30 Great Stories for Our Century

Adam Pfeffer

iUniverse, Inc.
Bloomington

30 Great Stories For Our Century

This is a work of fiction. All of the characters, names, incidents, organizations, and dialogue in this novel are either the products of the author's imagination or are used fictitiously.

iUniverse books may be ordered through booksellers or by contacting:

iUniverse
1663 Liberty Drive
Bloomington, IN 47403
www.iuniverse.com
1-800-Authors (1-800-288-4677)

ISBN: 978-1-4759-0446-8 (sc)
ISBN: 978-1-4759-0447-5 (e)

Printed in the United States of America

iUniverse rev. date: 3/23/2012

Where sky and water meet, there the earth is born.

ALTON "DOC" J. BLISS

CONTENTS

HEADS WILL ROLL

HORNSBY KERN MADE MOST of his fortune inventing a contraption known as the lunch-counter belt. It caught on in the late 1980s as a way for frantic businessmen to eat their lunch while scurrying to and fro. It was simply a piece of thick foam core board mounted to two canvass belts that fit about the person much like a pair of suspenders. On either side of the board were two small impressions the size of cups with a much larger impression in the middle enabling the consumer to carry a large dish of food. In its first year alone, I think the lunch-counter belt grossed something on the order of three million dollars.

I first met Hornsby Kern through an old writer friend of mine, Harry Twiggle. Although his one major novel sold over one million copies just a few years ago, Twiggle is still better remembered today by his moniker of the early 1960s, "The Fifth Beatle." You see it was Twiggle who was responsible for cleaning the Beatles' shirts after their initial Shea Stadium concert and later went on to write that mammoth best seller, "I Want to Wash Your Shirts."

One of my favorite excerpts from Twiggle's book was a paragraph about that historic day. "As the last screaming fans exited Shea Stadium, John Lennon stood about 300 feet below busy unbuttoning his shirt in the New York Mets locker room. Due to the commotion, his shirt was covered with stains. I still can remember John remark to me as he handed me the dirty shirt, 'Sorry about that last bit of coffee, Harry. I don't know what we would do without you.' Then Paul handed me a bottle of bleach. 'Harry,' he said, 'it's yo' turn to perform.'

1

As I said, Twiggle's book sold over a million copies and was the rage among Beatle fanatics even more than twenty years after the fact.

Anyway, Twiggle first introduced me to Hornsby Kern at a taping of Kern's new TV show, "Heads Will Roll." The premise of the show was to feature mock-interviews with great historical figures who had died by having their heads chopped off. It went on to become, as you probably will remember, a very popular show in the ratings for some time. Some of the famous people interviewed for the show were John the Baptist, Marie Antoinette and once, a live hook-up to Denmark was set up to talk to poor Yorick of "Hamlet" fame.

The show appeared on the Scuba-Diving Channel, a cable television network Kern had purchased with some of the funds he had gained from the lunch-counter belt. Kern subsequently appointed himself chief programming director of the network and placed his brother, Sony, in charge of all entertainment productions. Twiggle had brought me to the studio that day to help negotiate a contract with the Kern brothers to script a new show called, "Underwater Poker."

Upon entering the studio, Twiggle and I were ushered to two canvass chairs positioned in front of a small monitor. A man in a pinstriped suit wearing a cinnamon lunch-counter belt sauntered over to us with a wide smile flowing across his face.

"Hello, Harry," he said, still beaming, as he extended his hand in Twiggle's direction.

"Hello, Hornsby," Twiggle replied. "I want you to meet a friend of mine."

"Hi, Hornsby Kern," the man said, seemingly squeezing the words between his locked teeth. "Glad to meet you."

After briefly talking about Twiggle's subsequent writing contract, I asked Kern about the derivation of his strange name.

"I was named after the baseball player, Rogers Hornsby, who was a great hitter with the St. Louis Cardinals in the 1920s," Kern replied. "Won two Triple Crowns, Hornsby did, in 1922 and 1925 leading the National League in batting, runs batted in and home runs."

Kern paused for a moment. "I was a lot better off than my brother, I can tell you that," he suddenly said. "He was named after our television set. Sony Kern, they call him. Yep, father was there watching the TV when the call came from the hospital that my brother had been born.

Just sitting there watching the television. Told my mother he was too tired to go to the hospital."

Kern lit a cigarette, glanced up to survey his audience, and continued. "She ended up going with Aunt Catherine, who was named after an empress of Russia who supposedly died trying to have intercourse with one of the royal stallions. At least, that's what I once read."

"Anyway, father was sitting there in front of the television when he got the call from the hospital," he said.

"After telling him about his new son, my mother asked him for an appropriate name. There was a good show on at the time, and apparently it was distracting father. So when my mother asked him for a good name, father just said the first thing he could think of so as not to miss too much of the program."

"Sony, I remember him saying to this day. I was in the room at the time watching the same show. Although I don't remember now what the show was about, I do remember that old Sony television set we had. It was a fine set."

At this, Kern stood up and called his brother over. He was a tall man with an elongated jaw and sideburns that seemed to be dripping down his face.

"Hello there," Sony said, shaking our hands.

"Heard you were named after a television set," I said smiling.

"Yeah, quite appropriate don't you think?" he replied.

"Yes, I guess I do. By the way, what did your father do for a living?" I asked.

"My father worked for a TV dinner company in New Jersey. He was the man who pushed the buttons for the mashed potatoes section of the dinners," Kern said.

"He was very dedicated to his work which is why he said he watched so much television," Sony chimed in.

"Yes, he said his work demanded him to watch a certain number of television hours so that he could determine which dinners would be best to eat in front of each program," Hornsby agreed. "You could tell how serious he was about these studies for if anyone said a word during a particularly good program, father would immediately get very angry. 'Shhhhh, the mashed potatoes aren't ready yet,' he would say. We would quiet down real fast so as not to disturb father's work."

"My mother, meanwhile, also watched a lot of television, although she was always quick to point out how harmful the rays were to our eyes."

Sony nodded in agreement and then said, "My father, however, would always say the rays did not affect his eyes because he worked in the business."

"I never knew what being 'in the business' meant until I became the chief programming director for the Scuba-Diving Channel," said Hornsby.

At this, he and Sony got up and walked over to a corner of the studio where a monitor was showing a replay of the "Heads Will Roll" show. They came back shortly, although this time Hornsby wore a look of distress.

"Everybody's in just too damned a hurry," he finally said.

"Pop was right," Sony agreed. "He always used to tell us, 'Now in the good old days, it took a good fifty-four minutes to finish off one of those dinners. People had to be patient, check the dinner every fifteen minutes and gently place their fingers in the mashed potatoes to see if they were hot and smooth enough. But now they just zap the hell out of these things in one minute in their microwave ovens and shovel it down their throats in no time at all. Nobody appreciates the work that goes into producing TV dinners anymore."

"Everybody's in just too damned a hurry," Hornsby repeated once again invoking his father's favorite finishing words.

"Oh well," he finally continued after a long pause, "at least, that's what made me think of the lunch-counter belt." He tapped the cinnamon contraption lying next to his feet for emphasis.

"What about the show?" I asked.

After a long sigh, Hornsby replied, "Oh, the show will be okay. I think we'll have Goliath on next week."

"Yeah, when it's time to retire," Hornsby continued, "I'm going to take all my money and buy Yankee Stadium to house all the homeless people I can find. You know, all it needs now is a roof and it would be perfect."

We were quite taken with Hornsby's empathetic words and sat motionless as he suddenly produced a large set of stapled papers.

"Now Twiggle," he finally remarked, "what about this 'Underwater Poker' thing?"

THE STORM

"There is a storm," I said.

A pause.

"I don't see the idea of going to town, anyway," she said. "Shall we take anything to drink?"

"I'll get some whiskey," I said.

"Hope it was a good year," she said smiling.

"It's certainly not a good night to be outside."

"We'll be warm and drunk in a moment, anyway," I said.

"That's good," she said, "the storm is getting worse."

"It is, isn't it?" I said.

"That whiskey is good," she said.

"Oh, look, the storm is getting worse," I said.

"Lucky we didn't go to town," she said.

"You're a musician, aren't you?" I asked.

"Why, yes … why, how did you know? I'm a violinist. That's another reason, of course, why I decided to come to New York. I hope to give a recital here someday – perhaps at Carnegie Hall. It's thrilling to be in a big city like this, isn't it?"

"It is wonderful to live in a place like New York," I said.

"Oh, the storm is getting worse," she said.

"Yes, and the whiskey is getting better," I said.

"You're really very nice," she said.

"And you, my dear, are always a pleasure to be with," I said. "Even in the worst weather."

We kissed.

"Finish your whiskey, my dear," I said smiling.

She smiled.

We kissed once again.

"I want you to marry me," I said softly.

"What?" she said.

"I mean it."

"I know, if you say so," she said.

"You believe me?" I asked.

"I don't know what I believe," she said. "Oh, the storm is getting worse."

"Look, I didn't mean to catch you off guard," I said. "But I mean what I say."

"I know," she said.

"Have some more whiskey," I said.

"Don't you think we should make sure all the windows are closed?" she asked.

"Yes, good idea."

"Are you really in love with me?" she asked.

"Oh, if Heaven itself had but willed it!" I replied.

She could not help smiling.

"Why don't we sleep on it?" I said. "Why don't you take the couch?"

"You don't mind?"

"No, not at all," I said. "Listen, you don't think I'm drunk, do you?"

"No, not at all," she said.

"See how the wind is blowing straight across the river? That means there's going to be some flooding. You might as well get comfortable."

There was a glowing fire in the fireplace.

"Have another drink?"

"Why not?"

"See? And you thought I was drunk."

She smiled.

"Maybe I am," she said.

"You know you have a beautiful body, my dear," I said.

"You're very kind," she said.

"That whiskey was very good."

"Yes, a good year it was."

"Shall we gain some peace on earth?"

"Peace."

"You can always change your mind."

"Can I?"

"No."

"I'm glad."

The wind and rain swirled about outside. They walked together with their backs to the moon.

THE GENIUS

HE WAS A GENIUS. There was no doubt of that. He knew everything handed down through the ages, and could quote verbatim from any text. Nothing escaped his vibrant and inquisitive mind. Nothing. But there was more. He was creative and imaginative, writing and drawing from an original point of view. Yes, he was a genius of the very highest sort.

Then, one day, a strange man came to his door. He was dressed in black with a black fedora hiding a wild tuft of black hair. There was an anxious look on his face, as if he was searching for something, and his mouth was frozen in a questioning grimace.

"Are you the one?" he asked with a nasal sneer.

"I don't know what you mean, sir, although Diogenes was said to be looking for an honest man as he held a lantern…"

"Then it is you, isn't it?"

"That depends on the exposition as expounded by the expositor…"

"What is your name, lad?"

"The moniker given to me by my progenitors was Pi Wald."

"Yes, yes, Wald, that is the name."

Without another word, the strange man in black barreled into the room surveying all that was hidden inside. He took note of the many books on the many shelves and the notebooks and drawings lying scattered on the tables and floor.

"But who, may I ask, are you?" asked Pi Wald.

"Me? Why I'm the Genius Investigator, the one they alert when they think there is a genius in their midst."

"Genius Investigator? Why that's utterly absurd."

The strange man in black halted at the mention of the word, absurd, and gazed at the young man standing before him in a white shirt and droopy black pants.

"Absurd, did you say?" he finally questioned. "What do you know about it?"

"Why, as God is my witness, I have never been privy of any entry informing me of the existence of such a man."

The strange man in black stared at the young man with a mysterious grin. "And why, may I ask, did you bring God into the conversation?" he finally hissed.

The young man looked at him and smiled. "I don't know," he answered. "It just seemed appropriate at the time. Now if there are no further questions, I would really like to get back to my own investigation into the causes of the Reformation."

The strange man in black stood staring at the young man, and then suddenly, began to laugh. It was a long, steady laugh filled with grand guffaws and intermittent snorts of derision.

"And you call yourself a genius," he sniffled.

"I have been known by that complimentary term for many years," he replied. "Some, however, choose to use it as a term of violence. Which, sir, is your choice?"

"Neither as weapon or compliment," he replied. "You see, I think of the word as a term of fantasy, a mythological being that doesn't exist in the annals of history."

"But there have been certain people, such as Newton, Einstein and Shakespeare, who embody this concept."

"True, true," smiled the strange man in black. "These men certainly excelled in their chosen fields. But a complete genius is something entirely different. You see, to begin with, all these men believed in God and hoped to further the progress of the human race."

"Yes, and so?"

The strange man in black looked at him and smiled once again. "Well, as you will know in a few years hence, God was found to be an irrational belief based upon mythological thinking and lacking in evidence and sensibility. I believe you used the word, absurd."

"What do you mean by a few years hence?"

"You see when word filters down that a genius has arrived, well, it's my job to seek this person out and find out whether he or she really has the goods. You, I'm afraid, will not do."

The young man glanced at the strange man in black and shook his head. "You don't expect me to believe that, do you?" he asked.

"Strange that the human race does not believe in things it should, and yet, clings to a belief that there is some superior Being who is seeking to add meaning to the world according to some grand plan."

"But even if there is no God, there is some semblance of order in the world through superior natural forces," said Pi Wald.

"But there is no real order," argued the strange man in black. "Everything is rather arbitrary. I mean, I can choose to shoot you at this moment if I wanted to, ending your life and influence on the world."

"Then you're saying my life has meaning."

"No, not really. You see, your influence lasts for a very short time, and then eventually, you are forgotten like all the rest."

"But look at all the things humankind has done through the centuries," argued Pi Wald. "Surely, this has some significance."

"And if the human world ended tomorrow, would it still have significance?" asked the strange man in black. "Is it only significant among the adherents of the beliefs and history?"

"But look at the advances we made."

"And do they really have any significance?"

"But there's progress—"

"And there are continual wars and individual conflict—"

"But there are books and learning—"

"And there are misguided notions and simplistic morals—"

"But there's science and medicine—"

"And there's old age and eventual death—"

"But what about technology and convenience?"

"And there's money, ego and competition—"

"Then what are we supposed to do?"

The strange man in black grinned. "Nothing you can do," he finally said. "You see, we have found there really is no significance to anything the human race has done. We have found that at the end of the world nothing really matters much. All the names, all the accomplishments, all the words simply fade away to nothingness. We have found there is no God and never has been. It was all just words and superstition."

"Is that your destination?" asked Pi Wald. "The end of the world?"

"That is where I am from," replied the strange man in black. "When we heard there was a genius on the planet, I was sent to investigate. But you really know nothing, Pi Wald, isn't that correct? I mean, you mouth the words of those that came before, you know about the senseless history and wars fought for domination and the right to oppress, and you believe in that irrational Being we call God. No, no, that won't do. That won't do at all. No, no, you actually have very limited experiential knowledge, my friend, and inadequate opinions on life and the world around us. You see if you were really a genius, as they say, you would've known the absolute senselessness and inanity of life. Only after reaching this conclusion would you have known what to do. Alas—"

"Then that is all there is?" asked Pi Wald. "I don't believe it."

"It is your choice to believe anything you choose, however ridiculous or hurtful it may be. But because of what you believe and what you don't believe, you are not the one we are seeking."

"Then let me recrudesce my studying of the Reformation—"

"No, no, you won't do at all," murmured the strange man in black. "And I must be getting back to where I come from."

"Oh, yes," smiled Pi Wald. "And that would be the end of the world, correct?"

But there was no reply. When Pi Wald finally turned around, the strange man in black was gone.

THE HERMAPHRODITE

WHICH SEX, MALE OR female, experiences more pleasure during intercourse?

That's the question Zeus and Hera asked Tiresias all those years ago in Greek mythology. They thought Tiresias could settle the matter because he had lived as both a man and a woman. As a young man, a priest of Zeus, he found two snakes mating and hit them with a stick. He was suddenly transformed into a woman. As a woman, Tiresias became a priestess of Hera and a renowned prostitute. After seven years as a woman, Tiresias again struck mating snakes with her staff, and suddenly became a man again. Because of these experiences, the question was asked by Zeus and Hera.

Which sex, male or female, experiences more pleasure during intercourse?

Zeus said it was women. Hera claimed it was men. Tiresias was asked to settle the matter.

Tiresias finally replied that Zeus was right. He further explained that on a scale of one to ten, women enjoy sex nine times to men's one. Hera didn't take the answer very well. She struck Tiresias blind. When Zeus couldn't undo the curse, he gave Tiresias the gift of prophecy.

I am thinking about the old myth as I look down on my tits and penis. Yes, that's right, I have both. And a vagina, too. I am what you call a herm. A hermaphrodite. I was born with the sexual organs of both male and female. I am a gender all to myself. A hermaphrodite. My name is Jamie Figg.

It's not easy being both male and female. People are accustomed to

12

human beings being one or the other. I am both. It is a rarity to be both. The doctors can't even explain it. According to their precious statistics, about one percent of live births exhibit some degree of sexual ambiguity. I am that one percent.

So the question remains. Which sex, male or female, experiences more pleasure during intercourse?

I don't think Tiresias was entirely right. You see, in my experiences, I have enjoyed sex as much as a man as I have as a woman. The experience is different to be sure, but both are ultimately enjoyable.

I first discovered my unique nature at a very young age. I was about six and was rubbing my penis, when I felt myself getting wet underneath. My hand slid past my penis and balls, to the area between my balls and my asshole. It was so wet there, and it felt so good. I remember sliding my hand down toward the wetness, and discovering a small slit near my asshole. I put my finger in it, and it opened wider. I slid my finger inside and it opened into a small hole. I was scared and excited at the same time. I mean, it felt so good, and yet, I knew there was something wrong.

As I slid my finger further into the small hole, all of the anxiety seemed to melt away. There was a rush of euphoria, and then I took the finger out and smelled it. It didn't smell bad. On the contrary, it smelled like flowers. Flesh flowers.

Since that first feeling of euphoria and excitement, I have explored that small hole many times. As I got older, I couldn't believe how wet I would get down there. After sliding my finger in a few times, there would be such a thick stream of wetness that my dick would get very hard and straight, and finally send a geyser of sperm spurting onto the sheets.

I didn't know what to do or who to tell. I wondered if my mother knew. She must have noticed something when I was very young, but never said anything to me. I wondered myself what I should be, a male or a female. I didn't think people would allow me to be both. I decided I would be a male.

It was shortly after I made this decision that I was looking through a book on Greek mythology when I came across a passage about Hermaphroditus. He was the child of Aphrodite and Hermes, a handsome boy who became a hermaphrodite because of the nymph

Salmacis. He had been raised by nymphs on the sacred mountain of Mount Ida. At fifteen, he decided to travel to the cities of Lycia and Caria. In the woods of Caria, he came to a pool where he met Salmacis the Naiad. She tried to seduce the boy, but he rejected her. When he thought she had gone, he began taking off his clothes to swim in the pool of water. It was then Salmacis sprang out from behind a tree and jumped into the pool. Wrapping herself around the boy, she began kissing him and calling out to the gods that they should never part. Her request was granted, and the two bodies became one. Hermaphroditus was devastated. He cursed the pool so that anyone who bathed in it would also be transformed.

I put down the book and become aware of the pulsing under my balls. I am Hermaphroditus. The story was about me. I get up and walk to the bathroom. Turning on the water, I begin preparing my bath. Anyone swimming in the pool will also be transformed. Yes, for me the story is true. I am male and female in one body. Hermaphroditus.

I pour some shampoo in the bathtub and stir the water with my foot. Bubbles blossom amid the warm water. I step into the bath and sit down. My body aches. I lay back in the water and let the bubbles overtake my body. I am beginning to relax. I open my eyes underneath the water and the bubbles look like huge icebergs overhead. I sit up and watch the bubbles slide down my body toward the warm water below. I examine my chest and see that I have two swellings, the nipples erect. I look down and see my erect penis emerge from the tiny, white bubbles. There is a pounding, a swelling underneath my balls. I try to decide which part of my body I should rub first.

I am in the midst of transforming. I am becoming a woman, yet I want to live as a man. I squeeze my breasts, and the nipples become hard and swollen. I gently pinch them with my fingers, sit back and sigh. I feel the tightening underneath. I must rub it, sink my fingers into it, let the wetness merge with the warm, bubbly water. Yes, I am a woman, and yet my dick is still erect and pulsing.

I am thinking about the first time I got fucked. My friend, Eddie, had come to my house. He knew I was strange, but Eddie didn't seem to care. I led him into my room, and we began to talk. After a while, Eddie said he was hot and wanted to change into a pair of shorts. I sat on the bed and watched Eddie take off his pants. There was a huge bulge in his underwear. For some reason, he took off his underwear, baring the red, bulbous dick hiding underneath. He stood there with a huge erect penis straining toward the ceiling. I didn't know what to do. I felt myself getting wet underneath. I laid back on the bed and smiled.

"Yes, that's very nice, Eddie," I said.

Then I got up and walked over to him. I grabbed his erect penis with one of my hands and kissed his dick hole. It was warm and wet, and strained to attention. Then I put the red, bulbous head into my mouth. I sucked the head and then let it slip from my lips. Eddie had his head back, sighing with muted excitement. I held his dick in my hand, and then put it back in my mouth. My mouth slid down to the tan band around his penis. When I pulled his dick from my lips again, viscous liquid stretched from my mouth to his dick. The little strings of pre-cum kept stretching, until I found myself back on the bed.

"I want to fuck you," Eddie moaned. "Take your pants off."

I struggled with my pants and shirt until I was lying in my t-shirt and underwear.

"Take it off," Eddie urged.

I took off my t-shirt, revealing my small tits and erect nipples. My chest was completely hairless.

"That's what I thought," Eddie shouted. "You're a bitch."

"You haven't seen everything yet," I warned him.

"What the hell do you mean? Take it off."

I slid my underwear down to my feet, exposing my small erect penis and balls.

"What the fuck is going on?" Eddie asked incredulously. "You have tits and a dick?"

"That's not all," I replied in a whisper. "I also have a pussy."

I spread my legs and let Eddie look underneath my balls. It felt hot and very wet.

"Holy shit!" Eddie shouted. "I don't fuckin' believe it. You're as hairless as a woman, but you have a dick and balls."

"Ignore them, Eddie," I pleaded. "Fuck my pussy."

"Damn right I'm going to fuck your pussy," he replied. "This is pretty unbelievable."

Eddie then got between my upraised legs, and he slowly pushed his huge, swollen dick inside my small, wet pussy. It was too much for me. I moaned with pleasure. I could feel my pussy suddenly open and swallow the pulsing member. Yes, he was inside me. I could feel his huge dick filling me up inside. It was the most wonderful thing I had ever felt.

"Yes, Eddie, fuck me," I shouted.

He groaned and kept pushing inside me. I could feel my eyes glaze, and then my vision soften. I was transforming into a woman, and felt the hot urge as his dick sank deeper inside me.

"Fuck me, Eddie, fuck me," I panted.

He leaned forward and began squeezing my small breasts. My nipples were swollen and erect. Eddie kept pushing his huge dick in and out of me. I began to moan uncontrollably.

And then something happened. I suddenly felt sperm squirting out of my own penis. It was a heavenly feeling. I was having an orgasm as Eddie kept sliding his dick in and out of my small pussy. And then I heard him moan, and I felt the warm wetness surge inside me. Eddie was coming inside my pussy.

My legs were now spread wide apart, my toes pointed toward the wall. I had totally surrendered, wanting only to feel the warm fluid flow through me. Eddie had opened my pussy, and turned me into a woman. The feeling was indescribable. Uncontrollable euphoria and then sudden calmness. I could feel my own sperm oozing across my stomach, and then I blacked out.

When I opened my eyes, I could see Eddie smiling at me. There was still sperm dripping from his penis as he slid out of my opened vagina.

I could feel the sperm shooting out of my penis as I open my eyes. I am back in the warm, bubbly water and the memory of Eddie and my first fuck as a woman has sent shivers of pleasure coursing through my body. I shudder. I could feel a stream of wetness oozing underneath my balls. I am having a double orgasm, and I could do nothing but pinch my erect nipples.

Which sex, male or female, experiences more pleasure during intercourse?

Unlike Tiresias, I am hesitant to answer. The pleasure is different, but both are enthralling, I murmur. One has the power of penetration, the other the intensity of submission. Both are feelings of ecstasy, intoxication, rapture. It is a scuffle of give and take. A hip wrestle where there are no losers.

When Eddie opened me, I could feel the power, the surge, the energy. It was as if I was being held in a hypnotic trance and Eddie was the master hypnotist. I wanted nothing more than to submit, obey his every command. The hot urge inside my pussy yearned for penetration. Yearned to be filled by his huge, pulsing dick.

And then again, there is the other side of the coin. I sit back in the warm, bubbly water and think about the first time I fucked a woman. Her name was Dori, and when we met I felt somewhat scared, somewhat frightened, that I wouldn't be able to perform. Assume the position of power. The power of penetration.

Dori, however, was ignorant of my fears. We hardly knew each other when she walked over to me unzipped my pants and pulled out my dick. This was the same room in which Eddie had fucked me as a woman. Dori began sucking me with ardor, and I would be lying if I said it wasn't a pleasurable experience. I was quite hard as Dori sucked me, but there was a wetness spreading underneath. I hoped Dori wouldn't notice, wanting to savor my first fuck as a man.

Apparently, I was pleasing her. Dori began hurriedly taking off her clothes. She had large, plump breasts and areolas the size of quarters. Swollen, erect nipples stretched out from the middle of each areola. Dori then pulled down her pants and panties and shoved her ass into the air.

"Fuck me," she moaned.

I looked down, staring into a surprisingly clean asshole, and wondering if she wanted me to fuck her in the ass. I pulled out my penis, which was small and erect, and tapped it against her asshole.

"Not that hole," Dori protested. "The other hole. The pink hole."

Dori wanted it doggy style up her vagina, and I was getting worried that my penis wouldn't be long enough for such a task. I clenched the muscles in my ass, and then slid my penis into Dori's vagina from the rear. Surprisingly, it slid in and out rather easily. I was beginning to feel the power. The power of penetration. The feeling swelled inside my head, and urged me to keep pumping my dick inside Dori's raised pussy. It was a feeling of ecstasy, euphoria.

After a while, Dori turned around and lay back on the bed. She wanted me to fuck her missionary style, finish me off in a hail of glory riding her in the position most popular among couples. I willingly complied. I got on top of her and slid my dick inside her. I didn't even feel my pussy underneath. The rush of power, of penetration, swelled inside my erect dick. As I watched her huge tits flop below me, I realized I hadn't taken off my shirt. I wondered what I would do if Dori saw the swellings on my chest.

Thank God it never came to that. Dori sat back and closed her eyes, gyrating to the rhythm of my penis. I began sliding my dick in and out faster and faster until Dori began to moan.

"Yes, that's the way I like it," she whispered. "Fuck me hard and deep."

I forgot all about my pussy and tits when I heard Dori's sighs. It was as if my pussy had closed up, allowing my dick to take over and enjoy the power I now had over a woman. I began to buck wildly. I then put my hands on Dori's tits and began squeezing and pinching her nipples, much like I would enjoy having a man do to me. She squealed with delight.

I kept pushing harder and harder, sinking my dick deep inside Dori's pussy. With deft muscle control, I found I could make my dick even longer than I thought possible. I kept fucking her, riding her into ecstasy, when I felt my pussy open up underneath. The wetness was dripping down into my asshole, and the feeling engulfed my whole body.

"Yes, fuck me," Dori was screaming. "Fuck my pussy."

Her words echoed through my head. Fuck my pussy. All I could think about, however, was my own pussy. How hot and wet it was. My dick was still erect and now was red and pulsing. I suddenly became aware of my tits, hiding underneath my shirt. My nipples were swollen and erect. I couldn't take anymore.

As Dori continued to scream, I felt the warm semen squirting out of my dick. It flowed inside Dori like a warm vanilla milk shake. Then I slid my penis out of her vagina, and fell back onto the bed. The orgasm was too much, my head becoming numb from the wild frenzy of elation. I looked at Dori, and she smiled. I could see her nipples were still erect. I had given Dori a violent orgasm, too.

"Oh, that was so great, Jamie," she murmured. "You were really terrific."

She still hadn't noticed anything different about me. I smiled and then lay back on the bed, knowing I had pleased Dori as a man. A man of power, of penetration.

"I hope you're not too tired," Dori was saying.

She put her hand on my chest, and began massaging me in slow, calm strokes. Then her hand suddenly stopped, and she looked at me as if she had just seen a ghost.

"What's wrong?" I asked as calmly as possible.

"Oh, nothing," she replied. "It just seemed as if you didn't have an ounce of fat on your body."

"Well, I try to stay trim—"

"It's just that, well, your chest is a little flabby, Jamie."

I smiled. "It's just a thing I have," I said. "Anything I eat goes right to my chest."

"Oh, that's strange."

Before I could say another word, Dori leaned over and quickly lifted my shirt. The sudden action made my tits jiggle.

"What the fuck is that?" Dori shouted. "I knew there was something strange about you."

"It's nothing, Dori. I told you whatever I eat goes right to my chest."

"Yeah, right. Those are goddamned tits, Jamie. You have a pair of fuckin' tits."

"No, Dori, please wait. I can explain."

"That is gross, Jamie. You have a dick and balls and two little tits on your chest."

"They're not tits—"

Dori began getting dressed, and then she hurried from the room. I never did see her again.

I sit back in the warm, bubbly water and think of Dori. She really wasn't the right woman for me, I finally decide. I needed a woman who was more understanding, more compassionate. Someone who wouldn't get upset over a little thing like a flabby, jiggling chest. Someone who would savor the experience, the experience of fucking someone of a gender that only included one percent of the population.

Which sex, male or female, experiences more pleasure during intercourse?

The answer is not so simple. If it is a question of orgasm, I have had them both as a man and a woman. The feelings are equally intense. I decide I will keep searching for the answer, making love to both men and women as both a man and a woman. Eventually, I will find the answer. Maybe Tiresias was right. A woman feels so much during intercourse. The pleasure of total submission and surrender. But, then again, a man feels the power of domination, aggression swelling through his body. The pleasure of strength and persuasiveness.

I think about Hermaphroditus. How absurd it was for him to get so upset over obtaining such a precious gift. The gift to have man and woman in one body. The gift to see life from both sides of the fence. The gift to feel the pleasure of submission, and yet, the power of domination. Yes, to be given a precious, priceless gift envied by the ages. The gift of being both man and woman in one body. Hermaphroditus didn't understand. How could he curse the pool for all to transform? How could he give away such a gift because of juvenile disappointment?

I decide I am not like Hermaphroditus at all. No, I would be content with such a gift. I would seek out the differences between the sexes and explore the pleasure inherent in both. I would go beyond Tiresias and revel in the pleasure of intercourse as both a man and a woman. Only then would I finally come to an answer. Only then would I decide which sex I wanted to be. Only after careful and thorough experimentation.

There was suddenly a knocking at my door. I answer and see Billy Squonk standing there, looking as if he had no idea where he was or what he was doing.

"Come in, Billy," I finally tell him. "I'm really glad to see you."

Billy smiles, and then he steps into the light. He is a handsome man and his blond hair glistens in the light. His skin has that clean look one sees in the pages of magazine advertisements. I look into his blue eyes and smile. Billy makes me want to be a woman, makes me want to lie back in submission and feel his rigid dick inside. We have never made love before, but I decide I will change that. I admire his muscular chest and shoulders, and decide I will make love to Billy Squonk. The only problem is I am currently living as a man. Billy has no idea what I am hiding beneath my ordinary clothing.

"I thought maybe we would go drinking tonight," he says. "Maybe hook up with a couple of babes."

"Great idea," I say, not wanting to give myself away before a few drinks. "But I bought a bottle of wine, really good wine, and I thought maybe you'd give it a taste before we go."

"All right," Billy says. "Bring it on."

I open the bottle of Chardonnay and pour two glasses of sparkling white wine. Billy is still smiling as he takes the wine glass from my hand and downs half the Chardonnay in one gulp.

"Hey, that's not bad," he says, holding the glass in front of him. "It tastes like it was a good year."

"A very good year, Billy," I say, sitting down on the couch. "Relax, we have plenty of time."

Billy sits down next to me and takes a sip of the wine. I drink down half of my own wine and then look at him with an alluring smile. I can see Billy getting nervous, wondering why I am smiling like that.

"You know, there's so much about me you don't really know, Billy," I say, moving closer. "I mean, we've never really talked about each other much."

There's an awkward grin across Billy's face. I decide I won't keep him in the dark much longer.

"What the hell are you saying, Jamie?" he asks, suddenly eyeing the door.

"I've decided I want to be honest with you," I tell him. "You see, I'm not what I pretend to be."

"What the hell does that mean?"

"I hope you won't get upset, but look for yourself."

It is then I put down my glass and pull my shirt open, exposing my small jiggling tits. Billy takes one look, and then bolts backwards, as if some alien being has just popped out of my chest.

"Don't be upset, Billy," I say to him. "I was just waiting for the right moment to tell you."

"B-But those are tits," he stammers.

"Yes, Billy—"

"B-But I thought you were a guy."

"You never thought there was something strange about me?"

"W-Well, yeah, but I know a lot of strange people—"

"Billy, I like you. I want you to know that."

I lean over and put one hand on his cock. I can feel it through his pants, getting hard and swollen. Then I kiss him on the mouth and smile.

"B-But I-I thought—"

"It doesn't matter what you thought, Billy," I say to him. "What's important is that you now know the truth."

"You're kidding," he says, finally calming down. "I mean, all this time you had a pussy?"

"Yes, that's right, Billy. I have a pussy."

"But why didn't you tell anybody?"

"Because I wanted to know what it was to live like a man, Billy. I wanted to know who experiences more pleasure, a man or a woman."

He looks at me and smiles. "And what did you find?" he asks.

"I don't know," I say. "I'm still trying to find out."

"Well, maybe I should help you," he says with a grin. "Maybe you just need the right man to help you decide."

I smile. "I was hoping you would say that," I tell him. "But, you see, it's not so simple. There's more to the story."

"More? Like what?"

"Well, you'll never believe me. I have to show you. I just hope you're the person I think you are. That you won't make harsh judgments before thinking about it for a second. Oh, Billy, please try to understand—"

"Understand what? Are you a woman or aren't you?"

"Let me show you, Billy, and then you decide."

I stand up and turn my back to Billy. I then begin taking off my shirt. It's like a little show, a magic show, that I hope Billy will find pleasing. I always thought he would be the right one to show myself to. I turn back around and show Billy my small tits. The nipples are swollen and erect.

"Yes, those are nice, Jamie," he says. "I don't know why I didn't figure it out before."

"The show's not over yet," I tell him, shaking my finger. "There's still so much more to come."

I turn my back to him again and pull down my pants. I then slide my underwear down to my feet and kick it a few feet away. I bend over, letting Billy see my asshole and pussy from behind.

"What do you think, Billy?" I ask.

I turn my head and see Billy is behind me, standing only in his underwear. I smile back at him.

"Fuck me, Billy," I say to him. "Fuck my pussy."

Billy smiles back at me, and slides his underwear down to the floor. I can see his huge, erect penis throbbing behind me. He has the largest head I've ever seen on a penis. A giant Roman helmet.

"Let me see if I can take care of your problem," he says. "I never would have guessed you had such a nice pussy hiding underneath."

"Yes, and it's all for you, Billy—"

Before I can finish the sentence, I feel Billy's huge cock sliding inside me from behind. He is fucking me doggy style just as I had fucked Dori all those years ago. I try to decide which feels better, fucked from behind as a woman or doing the fucking as a man. Both are pleasurable, both produce utter enjoyment and euphoria.

"Let's do it Leapfrog style," Billy says, still pumping me from behind.

"Leapfrog?" I ask.

"Put you face down and your ass up in the air," Billy explains.

As long as I don't have to turn around, I will not protest. I will perform any position Billy wants as long as he's behind me. I place my head on the bed and my ass up in the air for Billy to fuck.

"Like this, charming Billy?" I ask.

"Perfect," he replies.

Billy slips his penis back inside me, and begins bucking. I am resting on the bed thinking what I should do if Billy wants me to turn around. For the moment, however, I enjoy the frenzied rocking. One thing is for certain: there's not as much work being a woman during intercourse. The man enjoys doing most of it. The power of penetration.

I feel Billy inside me, and the hot urge underneath my balls. He is fucking me in a frenzy when he suddenly stops.

"How about if I finish you off in the Yawning position?" he asks.

Billy is obviously a stud. He seems to know every sexual position invented by human beings.

"What's the Yawning position?" I ask him.

"Well, turn around, lie back, and spread your legs straight up in the air and wide apart," he tells me.

Sounds like a wonderful position to really get fucked hard and deep, except for me to perform it, I'd have to turn around. I don't know whether Billy is ready yet or not.

"Let's do it froggy style, Billy," I finally say, although I'm not really sure how the froggy position differs from the Leapfrog position.

"No, I want to look at you when I cum," Billy says. "I want to know it's you and ask myself why I didn't know all this time. What a royal waste of time not knowing. There's a lot of time to make up."

"But Billy, you don't understand—"

"I knew there was something wrong," he replies with a shake of the head. "I couldn't have been that stupid."

"You're not stupid, Billy—"

"What's going on? Turn around, Jamie."

I sigh, and then decide he would find out sooner or later. I might as well know now whether I'd be fucking Billy again.

"Okay, cover your eyes," I say.

"What the hell is going on?"

"Cover your eyes."

As Billy covers his eyes, I turn around and throw my legs straight up into the air and wide apart. The Yawning position. He then takes his hands away from his face, looks at me, and smiles.

"Okay, what's the surprise?"

"Oh, nothing."

He's about to slip his dick back in when he sees it. My dick and balls.

"What the hell is that?" he shouts. "I knew I couldn't be that stupid."

"It's okay, Billy," I assure him. "It's just that I have both. A pussy and a dick."

"Both?" he says.

"Both."

Billy looks at me and starts laughing. He is taking it much better than Dori.

"You waiting for a sex change?" he finally asks.

"No, I was born with both. I really am very lucky. I am part of only one percent of the population."

"Both. You know you should be in the world record books."

"Want to join me?" I say with a smile.

"Damn right," he says.

Billy starts fucking me in the Yawning position, and I sit back and enjoy it. My small dick is erect, but Billy doesn't mind. I can feel his sperm inside me, and then he takes his penis out and begins to hoot.

"Best fuck I've ever had," Billy says. "You really are the eighth wonder of the world, Jamie, my friend."

I smile, deciding that people like Billy will make my decision that much more difficult. Which sex, male or female, experiences more pleasure during intercourse? Right now, Billy is making me lean toward women, but my search is far from over. There is still so many people to meet, so many positions to try out. I smile at Billy and decide he is a good place to start.

Dating Miss Dracula

I HAD LIVED WITH Peter for three months, our college days having ended only shortly before in the midst of the June heat. He was a kind enough person, willing to share most of the things he had collected over his four years away from home. I, in turn, shared with him, creating a most satisfactory living situation. We were quite considerate of each other's lives, and particularly in the case of women, we did everything possible to allow the other to carry on a relationship without any unnecessary interference. But all that changed within a few harrowing days that I will never forget until I leave this earth once and for all, and hopefully, without complications.

The autumn winds had first appeared, sending the gaudy shriveled leaves swirling through the gray sky as a portent of the coming winter, when Peter came home, as usual, and placed his backpack on the kitchen table. I glanced at him and noticed a wide smile pervading his face. It was unusual for Peter to look so content, although I would not say he was a depressed sort of person; it was just that he usually had a tendency to hide his emotions in a rather stoic manner.

Noticing the grin spreading across his face, I turned to him and asked what had happened. "Well, you wouldn't believe it," was his reply. "I met the most beautiful woman last night at The Blarney Stone. One that I think will change my life forever."

I smiled. "Don't you think you're jumping ahead just a bit," I said. "I mean, you just met her, right?"

"Yeah, but there's something about her. I can't quite put my finger on it, but she's definitely different from any other girl I've ever met."

"You seeing her tonight?" I asked.

He nodded. "I'm taking her to the best place in town. I don't want to mess this up."

"She sounds like a real find. Do you want me to leave you the apartment for tonight?"

He looked at me and smiled. "No, that's okay," he said. "I'm going to try to get her to take me back to her place."

We left it at that, and a few hours later, Peter was decked out in his best clothes, his hair slicked back and gleaming.

"Well, good luck tonight," I said, watching as he headed for the door. He looked at me, smiled, and then humming a familiar tune, he quickly left.

The hours passed, hours spent lounging on the couch and watching television. I began to wonder how Peter had made out, but when the clock finally struck midnight, I decided I would wait to hear about it in the morning and went to bed.

When I awoke early the next morning, I noticed Peter's door was still open and his bed undisturbed. I smiled, and walking to the kitchen, began to prepare breakfast. I was in the middle of cooking the eggs, when the door suddenly swung open, and Peter stepped inside. I turned off the stove, and smiling, walked towards him.

The minute I glanced at his face, I knew something was wrong. His eyes seemed darker than usual and his hair was a matted mess.

"You okay, roomie?" I asked, staring at his eyes.

He looked back at me, almost as if he was in a trance, and began murmuring through his lips. I couldn't understand what he was saying, so I grabbed his shoulders and began to shake him.

He calmly looked at me, and as if he was still in a dream, he spoke in a hollow voice. "She is the most incredible woman I've ever met," he said. "You wouldn't believe how incredible she is."

I was somewhat confused. "Then you're all right?" I asked.

A thin smile spread across his lips. "You bet," he replied, his voice still devoid of emotion. "That was one of the most incredible nights I've ever had. Beth is a wild woman, and I'm totally in love."

I began to smile, thinking he had had quite a night, when I noticed his neck. There were two small discolored marks right above his collar.

"How did you get those?" I asked, pointing them out to him.

His reaction was one of unconcern. "Oh, that," he replied. "Like I told you, Beth is a wild woman."

There was a disconcerting faraway look in his eyes, and I suggested he get some needed rest.

He looked at me, as if he were still somewhere else, nodded, and slowly shuffled to his room.

I had eaten breakfast, and gone out for a few hours, when I returned to the apartment. Peter was sitting on the couch and staring at the television.

"You all right now?" I asked him.

"Yeah, fine," he replied. "I just needed some sleep."

"Good, because you had me scared for a while."

"I told you Beth was a wild woman. She had me up all night."

"You seeing her again?"

"Of course," he said. "We're going out tonight."

"You'd better be careful," I said. "Those looked like nasty bite marks on your neck."

He laughed, or at least seemed to attempt to laugh. What actually came out was something like a dull snort. "You know how it is," he finally said.

That night, Peter went out with Beth once again. And again, he appeared in the morning rumpled and lifeless. I walked up to him and took another look at his neck. The two marks had become something like cuts, with a thin drying trickle of blood running down behind the collar of his shirt.

"You sure this girl is all right?" I asked. "I mean, she seems to be doing harm to you."

"Oh, come on, Bob," he said in a dull tone. "You know better than that."

I thought about it for a moment, and decided maybe I shouldn't get myself involved in Peter's personal life. I mean, maybe the girl had some kind of kinky fetish or something. It was something Peter would have to deal with, and so, I decided to forget about it and let him go on with his life. That is, until a few days later, when Peter came home one morning, disheveled as usual, but looking as if his skin was shriveling.

"Are you okay?" I asked.

"I seem to be melting," he replied. And then he looked at me. "She wants to meet you," he said.

Although it was unexpected, it was certainly welcomed. I sure wanted to meet her. Now I'm not superstitious or religious or anything, but something told me this was no ordinary girl. I never believed in such legends before, thinking them the product of fear and ignorance, but this woman was no doubt a vampire of some kind. *Miss Dracula.*

And so when Peter asked me to come along with him for dinner, I jumped at the chance. But there was no way she was going to add me to her collection. I decided I would come armed to the teeth, so to speak.

The first thing I did was run down to the store for some garlic. This I would put in my pockets, in case she tried to make a move on me. The next thing I did was buy a large cross, which I wore around my neck. There was no way I was taking any chances.

That night, I put on my nicest clothes and accompanied Peter to the nearby restaurant. She was waiting for us outside. At first glance, she looked rather normal, with long, dark hair, a tiny curved nose and dark, sensuous eyes. The dim light, however, prevented any further investigation. When she looked at me, I tried to smile, but a dull haze seemed to envelop me. I listened to her words as if standing in a tunnel.

"Peter didn't tell me you were so cute," she was saying.

Then she led us into the restaurant, and I attempted to regain my wits. Feeling hot and sweaty, I instinctively reached into my pocket and pulled out the garlic. I heard a distant gasp and a hiss, and then suddenly my head cleared. I was holding the garlic up towards my face, and Beth was heading away from me stooped and fearful.

"Just as I suspected," I said to myself. I then put the garlic back in my pocket, but decided to hold on to it in case I began to feel woozy once again.

When Beth saw that I had put away the garlic, she straightened up and began to smile. "Do you always carry around garlic?" she asked.

Peter seemed to have no idea what she was talking about.

I looked at her and nodded. "An old habit," I said.

We sat down and I began staring at Beth's eyes. They were round and dark, almost as black as a gloomy night. I suddenly noticed her eyes matched her clothes, which were also black.

"I guess we all have some odd habits," she said.

"That's what makes the world go 'round," I said with a smile.

Beth smiled back at me, and for the first time, I could see two tiny fangs at the corners of her mouth. I tried not to stare at them and went on talking.

"So, where you from, Beth?" I asked.

She paused for a moment. "Oh, from a small town in Europe," she finally said.

I looked at Peter, who seemed to be in some kind of a trance.

"You're very nice," Beth was saying to me. "I should like to kiss you."

I was somewhat taken aback by the remark, but soon found myself leaning over towards her. As her face approached mine, the cross I was wearing suddenly fell from out of my shirt and dangled before her. I heard her hiss for a moment, and then her head darted back.

"What's wrong?" I asked.

"I was startled by your religious pendant," was her explanation.

I was going to ask further about her reaction, but the food came. Beth had ordered a rare steak, which was now steaming and bloody. We ate in silence, and then when we were finished, I asked her if she would like to check her makeup.

"Is there something wrong?" she wondered.

I nodded, and then reached into one of my pockets and pulled out a small mirror. Beth gasped when she saw what it was, and when I pointed it in her direction, it reflected an empty chair where she was sitting.

"You must understand, I'm not feeling very well," she said, rising from her chair. "I hope you will excuse me."

I tried not to smile. "Is there anything I can do for you?"

"Peter will take me home," was her abrupt reply. And with that, she grabbed Peter's hand and began walking away.

I left a few bills and then followed them. There was no way I was going to let them out of my sight. I caught a cab and then watched as they finally pulled up to a small house on the edge of town. I saw them quickly enter the house, and then getting out of the cab, I waited. And waited.

It was five in the morning when Peter finally came out of the house. He looked worn and tired, but I ran up to him and asked him if Beth was sleeping.

"Nah, we were up all night again," was his reply.

I grabbed his shoulders and looked into his eyes. They were black, as black as midnight, and glazed over with one of those eerie faraway looks.

"Now listen carefully," I told Peter. "Have you ever seen Beth sleep?"

He shook his head. "When I leave, she's always still walking around," he replied.

I shook him by the shoulders. "Now listen, we have to go back in there and find out where she sleeps," I said.

"What do you mean?" he mumbled.

"Don't you notice something strange about her? I mean, we have to find out who she really is."

Peter stared at me impassively and I grimaced. "How do we get back into the house?" I asked.

"I left the door open," he replied.

Dashing inside the house, there was no sign of Beth anywhere. I searched for her for quite a while and then happened to look in the garage. As I opened the door, I could smell the fetid odor and spotted a black coffin sitting towards the side. I almost couldn't believe my eyes, still doubting the existence of such ancient legends. But there was no doubt a coffin was there, and the only thing left to do was to look inside.

I hurried back to get Peter, hoping that what I thought would occur would help revive him and break the curse forever. He followed me without a word, and when he finally saw the coffin, it was as if he was looking at some strange object he had never seen before. He stood there staring and silent.

I hurried back into the house and quickly found an old wooden table. Breaking off one of the legs, I rushed into the kitchen, found a knife, and began sharpening it to a point. Then I returned to the garage and found a hammer.

Hurrying back to the coffin, I looked back at Peter. He was staring into space, his body gaunt and shriveled. The lid of the coffin opened with a loud creak, and then I saw her lying there amid some dirt. It was probably the dirt of her homeland or grave, I assumed, and placed the stake in the middle of her chest. As I began banging, Beth suddenly opened her eyes and sneered. I looked at her and kept banging the stake into her heart. She suddenly began to hiss, shifted against the sides of the coffin, and then lay motionless in a decaying heap.

I stepped back and turned towards Peter. He was bending over, rubbing his eyes, the life surging once again through his body.

"Wow, that was pretty intense," he finally said, looking up.

"She was a vampire. You were under her spell."

"I knew there was something wrong that very first night," he replied. "But there wasn't anything I could do about it."

"Well, it's all over now. Hopefully, you didn't lose too much blood."

I put my arm around him, and then we walked back out of the house. In the distance, the sun was rising between the distant hills.

"That was a close one," he said to me with a smile. "I don't think I could've lasted much longer."

"You'll be all right, eventually," I assured him.

We both glanced at the rising sun, and then Peter began to groan. His body suddenly began to collapse, the snapping of bones piercing the morning silence. In the morning light, Peter's body began dissolving into a skeleton and then to dust. I stood staring at the white ash, and realized Peter had actually been dead for several days. Beth had probably taken too much blood that very first night, and Peter was nothing more than one of the walking Un-Dead. His soul now at rest, I walked back home in the growing sunlight.

THE LONG NIGHTMARE

Dedicated to Morris Siegelstein

BLACK SMOKE POURED FROM the five large chimneys, billowing upward, and gently tumbling into the luminous sky. Harry Berg, twelve years old, glanced at his older brother's face and dropped his hands to his side. Rows of prisoners stretched before him, each dressed in blue stripes and a thin metal strip attached to their wrists. Harry looked down. He was number 69589.

He could hear the German soldiers shouting in the distance. They were shouting in German, "Attention! Attention!"

He scanned the rows of prisoners standing in front of the shower barracks, their hair cut short and a one-inch wide part shaven off to identify them in case they chose to escape. There was an odd, putrid odor wafting through the air. He looked up and could see smoke spilling from the five large chimneys.

"Are they burning our clothes and shoes?" he whispered to his brother.

His brother, seven years older, looked down. "Quiet, you're going to get us in trouble," he whispered back.

Harry remained at attention, staring at the crematorium chimneys, smelling the foul stench emanating into the air, and listening to the German soldiers shouting in the distance, when he felt someone tap him on the shoulder.

"Your medication, Mr. Berg," the nurse was saying. "It's time for your medication."

Berg slowly opened his eyes, the glare beaming until it dissolved back into the light of his hospital room.

"Take these pills," said the nurse. "Lunch will be very soon."

He let the pills fall into his hand, and then, one by one, they slid down his throat with a gurgle of water. Much good they would do, he told himself. He knew he didn't have much time left.

"And how are you feeling today?" she asked.

Berg sighed. "The dreams, they've come back again. I was back at Auschwitz."

"Poor man," she replied. "How did people ever get that cruel?"

He watched her walk away, her buttocks moving beneath the tight, white uniform, and repeated the question to himself. *How did people ever get that cruel?*

He smiled. Because that's the way it's always been, he said aloud. Human nature, the cruelty of the beast that is man. He leaned back in the bed, thinking about the cause of human cruelty.

Well, in my case, he finally concluded, it's because I happen not to believe in Jesus Christ. Yes, that's it, isn't it? The whole ball of wax. The reason Jews have been mistreated through the centuries. We do not accept the majority's God. We do not accept him because he failed to bring peace and harmony to the world.

Berg sighed. And because of that very fact, he told himself, his people were burned to ashes in the ovens, doused with carbon monoxide and hydrogen cyanide, Zyklon-B, as they huddled naked within the walls of the so-called "showers," or taken to be experimented on by the hideous madmen purporting to be doctors. Oh, yes, he saw what happened to his people after the war; the emaciated bodies piled on top of each other in the mass graves, the human-skin lamps that were the envy of Hell, and the twins with pupils that no longer matched. *How did people ever get that cruel?*

He thought about it and laughed. *When were people not cruel through the history of man?* From the very beginning, he told himself, Cain killed Abel. Was that not out of cruelty and jealousy? Then came Noah, and the entire world was drowned. An entire world of cruelty. Yes, God knew it from the beginning. How appropriate that the majority's Savior was found nailed to the Cross. Was that also not cruelty? The blood thirst of the human race? And, of course, he sighed, it was his people, the Jewish people, who were eventually blamed for it. The people of the Hebrew God. The One God, invisible and omnipotent. He laughed once again.

There wasn't any proof that any God ever existed, and yet, people murdered each other at the mention of the word. Just an excuse to oppress one another, he nodded to himself. *An entire world of cruelty.*

He closed his eyes, leaned back, and fell wearily into the clutches of the past...

When he opened his eyes again he was back in the village of Verecky in the Carpathian Mountains of Ruthenia, a province of Czechoslovakia. It was the summer of 1941 on the ninth day of the Hebrew month of Av and the Czechoslovakians who had allowed the Jewish population of Verecky to practice their religion without restrictions were gone. As the German armies occupied the country, Hungarian soldiers filled the village.

Harry's father and others who could not prove they were born in the area were rounded up and assembled in the village's main square for deportation to Poland. It was the day Harry and the other Jewish residents were supposed to mourn the destruction of the Temple in Jerusalem, but instead, were faced with the separation of their families.

Harry watched as the Hungarian Police pushed his father toward a bus that would take him to Poland. His father fell and one policeman grabbed him by his black beard and dragged him to the vehicle. Harry ran toward his father, but when he reached the bus, he was also pushed inside. Harry's father picked him up and held him in his arms. They both cried uncontrollably.

"Please, he is only a boy," Harry's mother pleaded outside the bus. "Please do not take him away from us."

A policeman finally listened to her cries, stepped onto the bus, and seized Harry by the neck. He was still in the midst of hugging his father when he was pushed off the bus. That was the last time he saw his father alive.

He watched as the bus sped away and the Jews of the village assembled in the synagogue to sit on the floor and lament the destruction of the ancient Temple. They later heard the occupants of the bus were taken to a city in Poland where they were lined up and machine gunned to death by the Gestapo...

Harry Berg woke up coughing, feeling as if a knife had been plunged into his stomach.

"Mr. Berg, are you all right?" asked the nurse.

Berg stopped coughing, and looked up. "I don't have much time, do I?" he rasped.

"No one knows that, Mr. Berg," replied the nurse. "Were you dreaming again?"

He nodded. "Yes, the Nazis. The beginning of the *die Judenfrage*." Berg let out a sardonic laugh. "The final solution."

The nurse shook her head, and frowned. "Well, there's no one here who wants to do you any harm. We would just like to see you on your feet again."

He tried to smile. "We'll leave it to God," he finally said.

The nurse turned and walked away, and Berg began thinking about how it all began. Verecky. How he loved sliding to school on skis while being pulled by a horse-drawn sleigh in winter or the fragrance of the Lily of the Valley that grew in the meadows in the spring...The thought of the soldiers reemerged in his brain. 1941. Soon, they were forced to wear badges or armbands marked with a yellow star. *Juden*. In the following months, tens of thousands were deported to ghettos in Poland and to cities taken from Russia. He had heard later that the persecution of the Jews in Germany began in 1933, but to him, it all happened in a blink of an eye.

Die Judenfrage. It had been happening for years. Down through the centuries, ever since they had been pinned with the death of the Christian Savior. The Savior who walked among the Jewish masses of Nazareth and Galilee.

Even after the war, there were many who didn't want to even believe that it ever occurred. Did not want to know or care what had happened to the Jews and other minorities. *How did people ever get that cruel?*

Berg put his head down on the pillow and drifted back to sleep. The Americans were coming. He could see the Nazis retreating, jumping in their cars and trucks and speeding away, with the first glimpse of the American tanks. Millions had been slaughtered in their wake, most for no better reason than embracing religious beliefs that differed from theirs, and the few victims that remained still clinging to life were left starving amid the ravaged remains of their brethren.

He was sitting at the Displaced Persons Camp, where rumors of all types spread among those looking for any trace of living relatives. "I had been taken to a death camp known as Gunskirchen," said one man. "A terrible place, an absolute torture chamber. No sanitary conditions, never a change of clothing. For six weeks, we were subjected to complete starvation."

He stared into the man's hollow eyes, and sunken cheeks, and then gazed at the others, all the others subjugated by the cruelty of the world. A tear rolled down his cheek. "I have seen people drinking their own urine, dying by the hundreds," the man was saying. "None of the bodies were given burials and many were used as mattresses. There was cannibalism, death was everywhere. Then we heard cannon fire and we saw the SS guards jump onto their trucks and drive away."

The Americans had arrived, and with them, came food and comfort. He was lying in front of one of the soldiers when they first arrived, and the soldier reached down and handed him a can of baked beans and a can of condensed milk. They were alive. Alive...

"Mr. Berg, your lunch is ready."

It was the nurse, and he sat up, glancing at the meal, knowing it would never taste as good as those baked beans he was given years ago. He began to cough, and then the pain returned, and he sat back with a groan.

He was ready to go. He had survived the death camps along with his brother, had married, had raised his children, made a little money in the food business, and now he was prepared for death. A natural death. A legitimate death. He wondered if the world would ever forget what had happened to all those Jews all those years ago. Six million. A generation.

In time, they would fade with the passing years, and the world would once again engage in bouts of cruelty. They might not be as bad, maybe worse, but they would occur. Hadn't that been the way it was throughout human history?

Meanwhile, the survival of his people would be continually threatened. The ideal of a Jewish homeland to avoid the world's cruelty had come true, and now it was the object of disdain and disapproval. Would the world ever stop hating us?

Berg sighed, and closed his eyelids, wanting the faces of his wife and children to appear before him. He could see only a long, jagged path knifing its way into a tranquil white haze. A sudden pain jolted his body, and then he followed the path slowly towards the horizon.

A PRAYER

O LORD, HEAR ME, and only me, as I whisper my telepathic plea to you wherever you may be.

Please, dear Lord, protect me and bless me, although I may be obnoxious and insensitive to those around me.

Hear my prayer, O Lord, among the billions of people on this planet, no matter how immense or small you may be or your location, and help me attain all the things that, in reality, I don't really justly deserve.

Hurt all of those people who dislike me, O Lord, may they be enemies or friends, and do not listen to their versions of the truth, but turn a deaf ear to them and only listen to whatever I have to say.

Dear Lord, give me something for free so that I will know that you appreciate my taking the time to pray to you, although like most human beings I value money above all things. But give me something, dear Lord, many things out of the goodness of your heart and without remuneration.

Acknowledge to those who defy me how superior I am to other human beings, and allow me to punish anyone I choose, no matter if I am right or wrong, no matter if it is warranted or completely the product of sheer selfishness, and allow me to do it without any kind of retribution.

Thank you, O Lord, although you know me well, or at least what I tell you, and give me all kinds of things and happiness so that I may be able to buy and sell whoever and whatever I wish with the accepted fact that I am superior to others.

Bless me, O Lord, and let me grovel at your invisible feet so that you may allow me to defy Nature and reality and dictate to others my own sinful and immoral demands.

Degrade others, O dear Lord, and lift me up to the highest ranking so that I may disdain whoever I wish and eventually take over your throne.

Let us ignore reality, as we do whenever we talk about such things as Heaven, the Messiah, or any kind of divine plan or overall purpose.

Guide me, O Lord, so that I may make a fool of others and reach my unrealistic goals, even though my actions on Earth are vile and insidious.

Please, O Lord, disregard logic and justice, and arbitrarily favor me above all others. Justify my treatment of others and agree with my egotistical and self-serving opinions and ideas.

Let me criticize others, O Lord, although it be unfounded or cruel or based on my own violent and disagreeable nature, and grant me the grandeur of my dreams without any critical retaliation.

Thank you, Lord, for approving of everything I do and everything I want, and disregarding those I dislike, and preventing them from getting into Heaven because they don't see things the way I do or are different from myself.

Let me pray for others, dear Lord, although I know you only as well as anyone else on this planet, which isn't very well, I must admit, but give me special attention above all else so that I may despise and ridicule those who think you hear them as clearly as you do me.

I look forward to seeing you when you return to the Earth and favor my religion and ideas above all the other ridiculous religions, and afflicting them and destroying them unless they accept what I believe.

Thank you, dear Lord, until you return I will exhibit a false empathy towards others in remembrance of your brutal and barbaric treatment here on this Earth.

Love me, O Lord, and I will in turn give you the ultimate honor of my own irrational love. And let there be Peace on Earth, O Lord, unless I want to start something, which you will undoubtedly support without any questions asked.

Let me live a long and healthy life, dear Lord, although I don't deserve it, and heal me if anything goes wrong.

Grant me all things because I follow your alleged laws as interpreted by other human beings, and which you haven't expounded on since you last directly communicated with us thousands of years ago.

Thank you, dear Lord, I will be expecting what I want as soon as possible.

Amen.

LIFE AFTER DEATH

I HAD BEEN DEAD. That's right, dead as a doornail, as they say. I was sitting there at that fish restaurant my wife, Gena, likes so much when I suddenly began writhing and gurgling after ordering flounder. I usually like flounder, but this time, I began gagging, fell from my seat, and found myself staring into an endless darkness. It was then I felt as if my mind was a television set, and without warning, somebody came along and just turned it off. Nothingness. It was probably only temporary technical difficulties because the set turned back on, and I opened my eyes still staring into an endless darkness. I was lying on my back, my arms at my side, a soft cushion beneath my head. I felt relaxed, comfortable, as if I had slept for weeks. Then I yawned, and decided to sit up, wondering just where the hell I was. *Bang!* My head crashed into something wooden, and I fell back to the soft cushion.

My head now pounding, I reached out and began moving my hands all around me. I was surrounded by walls. Clenching my hand, I tapped at the ceiling, which was only a few inches above my head. It was definitely wood, thick and heavy. I began to get nervous, still in darkness, lying on my back, seemingly trapped in some narrow, wooden box. *And then it hit me!* This was a coffin I was lying in, and I had mistakenly been presumed dead. But, of course, that had to be it. Then I began to get nervous again, wondering if I was lying in some moldering grave, buried beneath mounds of dirt and rock. Gena wouldn't do this to me, I muttered to myself. But what if she thought I was really dead, checking out after sampling the flounder. I began to panic, and threw my hands against the wooden lid. I began banging with every ounce of strength, gasping with every breath. How could she do this to me? How was it possible for those moronic doctors to make such a serious mistake?

I was alive, there no doubt of that. I knew that was true when I smashed my fist against the wooden lid, and felt the pain racing through my body. But if somebody didn't find me soon, I really would be dead, once and for all. The air down here wouldn't last forever. My heart was pumping, there was no doubt of that, either. I could hear the blood pulsing through my body, the adrenaline soaring through my system. I planted my hands against the wooden lid, and began pushing with all my might. If I was buried alive, I was surely doomed.

As I pushed harder, I suddenly heard a loud creak, and then the lid floated out of my hands and groaned upward. Faint light gushed all around me, and I covered my eyes to protect them from the sudden onslaught. After a few moments, I blinked my eyes and stared into the fading light. It was apparently twilight, helping my eyes to adjust more quickly to the abrupt change in my environment. Thankfully, I had not yet been buried.

"Shit, there's going to be one helluva lawsuit," I mumbled, trying to stand up. My legs felt weak and my feet unsteady, as my head slowly rose from the darkness. When I finally got to my feet and pushed myself over the side of the coffin, I spotted a man in blue overalls walking towards me. As soon as he saw me, he stopped dead in his tracks and his mouth fell open. I watched as he stared up into the sky and crossed himself with a religious fervor that almost made me laugh.

"You look like a healthy specimen," I said, waiting for his reaction.

He looked at me, his eyes bulging wide, the faint light glowing in the whites of his eyeballs, and then he threw his arms up in the air as if he were stopping some runaway intruder from doing him serious bodily harm.

"Geez!" he screamed in a high-pitched voice that didn't seem suited for his wide, bulging neck. I almost laughed once again.

You've never seen such a pudgy man run so fast in all your life. He turned, like a swinging door opening, and raced away in little pattering steps. I watched him as he finally reached a nearby house, and darted inside. The sight of his waddling steps clung to my brain, and I finally threw my head back and burst out laughing. So it was true. I had been dead, after all. When I stopped laughing, I could see I was standing in the middle of a huge cemetery, tombstones, like little bald men, hunched all around me. I looked back at the coffin, the lid propped open, the dying light reflected in the gold handle and the buttery sheen of the wood. A pile of dirt was lying in front.

"I wonder if we'll be able to get a refund," I mumbled, smiling to myself. I then looked down and noticed my clothes for the first time. A wrinkled, dark suit and my good black shoes. Gena always knew how to dress me well for any occasion. I smoothed my hands over the black jacket, and thought about my next move. I had to try to get back home, and find out from Gena what had really happened, how things had changed while I was gone.

I took a step forward, staring at the house where the pudgy man in the overalls had run to, and wondered if I could convince him to give me a ride. Surely, he would eventually realize that the whole thing had been a mistake, and that I wasn't really one of the walking Un-dead.

It felt good to be moving my legs once again. You don't realize how weak you become without a little exercise now and then. I stared up into the sky. The light was almost gone. Maybe it was my imagination, but the moon looked like a pale skull hanging overhead. It was like some leftover decoration from Halloween, and as I trudged forward, I realized the man in the overalls thought the same of me. I kept walking, my eyes fixed on the light inside the house, when I felt an itch creeping down my right arm. I reached over with my left arm and began scratching. Something, however, didn't feel right. I looked down at my right arm and noticed flecks of skin curling up and flying into the growing darkness. *I must have been dead longer than I thought*, I murmured to myself.

When I finally reached the house, I began to knock. There was a shrill scream from inside, and then the sound of hurried steps. I kept knocking, and when that didn't work, began banging on the door. After a few moments, the door swung open and the pudgy man in the blue overalls was standing in front of me holding a large crucifix in the air.

"Go away, evil one," he was screaming in that unnatural high-pitched voice.

"No, you don't understand," I finally growled, losing my patience. "I need a ride home and you're the only one around."

He looked at me, let out another high-pitched scream, and then reached into one of his pockets. "Stay away from us," he squealed, withdrawing his hand from the pocket and then tossing a ring of keys at my feet.

"For that, you shall live, my friend," I said as seriously as possible without breaking up. "Now go and tell your loved ones, you have seen Death, and he let you pass."

He shook his head, attempting to smile, still holding the crucifix with stiff arms out towards my eyes. He then crossed himself, stepped backwards in quick, waddling steps, and slammed the door.

I was driving back home in an old Chevy, the exhaust rumbling like an angry god, and thinking about Gena. *Boy, did I have a surprise for her.* I pictured her, lying there on the sofa, sobbing away for days, and then having to wear those drab black clothes to let everyone know her partner, her lover, had been taken from her. What would she say when she saw me walking through that door without the slightest hint of a problem?

I watched the lights sweeping by as the car rumbled onward, and wondered what I would say. Would I play it for laughs or try to take it seriously? Then I pulled up the street, our street, and glided into the driveway. I looked up at the house, and noticed something was missing. The basketball hoop was no longer hanging above the garage door. I always loved that hoop to get a little exercise, and now it was gone. What else had she changed?

I thought about it for a moment, decided it was probably blown down by the wind, and shut the car engine. I opened the car door, slid out, and noticed the pathway leading up to the house was different. It was now inlaid with brick. Gena never did anything without getting my approval. Probably wanted to change the environment a little to deal with her unexpected tragedy. I looked up at the house, and studied the façade. It was our house all right, no doubt of that. The dent near the front window was still there which I accidentally created with the help of an errant hammer. Yep, definitely the right house.

I stepped up to the peeling white front door, and began knocking.

No answer. *Damn, where could she be at this hour?* Then, finally, there was the sound of footsteps. The door then swung open, and I could hear her gasp.

"Robert?" she shouted incredulously, as if in the midst of an enveloping nightmare.

I looked at her, worn and battered as the suit I was wearing, and tried to smile. "It's me," I finally blurted out. "I've come back, Gena. As difficult as it might be to believe, I've actually returned."

"But you've been dead for days," she said. I could hear her heart pounding. "How can it be?"

"Don't know," I replied after a brief hesitation. "But it is me, I do know that. It's like I've been sleeping, caught in some long, dark tunnel. Finally, I opened my eyes and realized I was lying in a coffin."

"That's because I buried you. You had a heart attack."

I looked at her, and tried my best not to smile. "I'm feeling fine now," I said. "Like I've slept for weeks."

I then stepped inside the house, could see she was still confused, and noticed some more skin falling off my right hand. "Guess I'll go get cleaned up. I must look like a wreck."

"Is this some kind of a joke?" she screamed. "Is that you, Thomas, just trying to scare me?"

Thomas was my best friend. He lived a few doors down. "I assure you it's me, Gena. I've come back from the dead."

I heard her scream once again, and fall limply to the floor. *Must have been some shock*, I thought to myself. I bent down, and lightly began slapping her face. After a few moments, she opened her eyes. She looked at me, sighed, and then seemed to begin accepting the reality of the situation. She slowly got back to her feet, and frowned.

"But you've been dead, Robert," she said, her voice somewhat trembling. "You didn't hear any voices, see anything?"

"Nothing but a long, dark nothingness. But I'm back again, Gena, and I've decided I'm going to use this second chance to make it up to you. Take you to those places I never seemed to find the time for. Buy you the things you always wanted, but I never could appreciate. I do now, Gena, my darling, and I'm sorry for all the pain I've caused you."

"But you've gotten a second chance. Why, Robert?"

I looked at her, and shrugged my shoulders. "I really can't say. Just one of those quirks of fate."

"Well. What do we do now?" she asked, looking at my wrinkled suit and my curling skin.

"Live like it's the last day of our lives," I said. "Whatever your desire might be, I'll make it come true."

When I first looked at myself in the bathroom mirror, I had a hard time believing what I was seeing. My hair was all matted and in knots, and my right eyeball seemed to be straining at the socket. Surely, I couldn't have been dead for that long a period of time. But, apparently, I had been. I stared at the skin curling up on my face, making me look as if I were suffering from an advanced case of leprosy, and tried to smile.

The Man Who Came Back From the Dead, I said to myself. Wait until the television reporters, the newspapers and the internet hear about it. *This is one story that is going to blow their minds.* I thought about it for a moment, and decided publicity was just a fleeting fancy. What I really wanted to do was make Gena happy once and for all. I realized how selfish I had been all those years.

The warm shower felt better than anything I had felt in a very long time. The water was soothing and seemed to revitalize my battered soul. I began whistling, and then singing old familiar tunes. I closed my eyes and thought about taking Gena somewhere she'd always wanted to go, but I had thought was too expensive or too inconvenient.

"Just you and me, Gena, the two of us, the way it always should have been," I would say.

Then she would grab my hand, and ask me why. "Because I've gotten a second chance at life," I would reply.

"I still can't believe it's true," Gena said, as I stepped out of the shower and brushed my hair. "Don't you think you've got some sort of responsibility to others to live a good second life and teach others the errors of their ways?"

"Whatever you think is best," I replied. "As I told you, this second life is going to be lived just for you, Gena. Whatever you think is right."

"I don't know what's right anymore, Robert. I mean, I don't know if it's right that you should get the chance to live a second life, considering the way you lived your first life."

"I told you I'd make up for it, Gena—"

"I don't know if it's right that you should get the chance," she replied.

As I watched her walk away, I thought about what she said. Maybe she was right. Maybe I didn't deserve a second chance. But someone somewhere seemed to disagree, and so I would accept it. If only Gena would, too.

I decided maybe a little publicity wouldn't be too bad to make Gena realize the value I now had. I would alert the media, and tell them all about how I got the chance to live again. Then maybe Gena would begin to appreciate the situation, and allow me to begin making her life more comfortable.

The reporters finally came with their cameras and their questions. They had a ton of questions to ask. They wanted to know everything from what I had for breakfast to what was the color of God's eyes. I tried to tell them what I knew, what I remembered, but it seemed as if it wasn't enough. They began laughing challenging me on certain details, and then decided I wasn't telling the truth. They didn't believe I had ever been dead.

I tried explaining it to them, tried to make them understand that not everything was so easy to explain, and then decided it wasn't worth it any longer. What did it matter if no one believed me? Now maybe I could live a good, clean life without any interference. Maybe all I needed to think about was how to please Gena.

They took their cameras and their sarcasm and they left me alone with Gena and the truth. It didn't matter to me any longer. Gena was the only one I had to convince that a second chance was very real and very worthwhile.

"They didn't believe you?" she finally asked, watching as they exited our home. "Well, what do we do, Robert?"

"Does it really matter, Gena?" I said. "I mean, I was thinking the publicity would do us good, but maybe privacy is a good thing. A good thing to do all the things we always wanted to do."

She smiled, and we began our quest for happiness. We first began by going to the jewelry store. I wanted to buy Gena a ring, a second wedding ring.

"We'll do it all over again, Gena," I told her. "And, this time, we'll do it right."

"But you never liked diamonds," she replied. "You always said they were simply expensive rocks."

"Forget about what I said," I smiled. "This time, I've learned my lesson and know that what I said before was just not true."

So I bought her the diamonds and I bought her the rings and the necklaces and she looked at me with a smile on her face, and I thought we would truly be happy. Yes, that's all I wanted – for us to be truly happy together.

But then we got home and the arguments started once again. Maybe I was only trying to trick her. Maybe I didn't really love her, but just wanted her to love me. Maybe I was just trying to make her happy so I could boss her around again. Maybe I didn't really die, but just found someone else to live with for a short time. The accusations went on.

I told her she was wrong about me, had always been wrong about me, and that I would prove to her in the coming weeks and months and years that I was really a good person who wanted to love her and be happy.

Then the night came, and she said she didn't trust me enough to sleep in the same bed. So I trudged off to the couch, my first night back in my home, and closed my eyes and hoped for a pleasant dream.

I was lying there, trying to remember what I might have seen while I was dead, and then heard the voices in the distance. A great mélange of sounds wafted through the room. Through the mist of sounds, I could now detect voices darting in and out in varying degrees of volume. They were the voices of those in pain, of those in the midst of some distant battle, of those struggling for an elusive identity.

I wanted to know if they were the voices of angels, of those just going to heaven, or of those preparing to do battle with those on the planet below. Then it hit me. Maybe they were the voices of demons, and this was not heaven I was thinking about, but maybe hell. Maybe I had been sent to hell before coming back to the land of the living.

"Yes, I have been very happy," said someone in the distance.

Was this God or the Devil himself? And why was I sent back to earth?

"Well, I prefer to call myself Lucifer. Like the ring of it, you know."

I shut my eyes tight and began to pray. I must have been sent to the demons below, I mumbled to myself. But why did they let me go?

"I am the Son of the Morning, the Prince of Darkness, the Enemy of Mankind, The Father of Lies, The Angel of the Bottomless Pit, The Dweller in Pandemonium. I am Old Scratch, Old Horney, Old Clootie, The Cloven Hoof, Old Gooseberry, Beelzebub, Old Harry, The Denizen of Hell."

Well, what did he want from me? I'm the first to admit I may not have treated Gena very well, but I never physically abused her. I never really verbally abused her. I might have told her what to do because I didn't really respect her judgment, but was that enough to be sentenced to hell?

Was that enough to be sent down below? But I got a second chance. They sent me back. Even the Devil knew it was wrong to put a man in hell who didn't actually deserve to be there.

Gena did worse than I did. She fought with me all the time, no matter what I did for her. If I was kind, she was suddenly cruel. If I tried to reason with her, she was angry and crude. That had to be taken into consideration, after all. No, a man was not an island unto himself. There were others involved who influenced the way he confronted certain situations. That had to be part of the equation. There were others involved.

Then I heard the voices of those of kindness, and of understanding, and thought maybe I had gone to heaven, after all. Yes, the angels knew I was a good man at heart. Yes, they knew I wouldn't do harm to anyone or anything. I was a good man, a gentle man, a man who would not kill a living thing if I didn't have to. I didn't hunt, I didn't keep pets out of a need for oppression or selfishness, and I cared about the world around me.

Yes, that was it, I had gone to heaven. After all, my biggest sin was catching a gleaming rainbow trout in a lake in the Sierra Nevadas. I didn't want to do it, I protested at the thought of it. But my friends said I had to do it on my own, and so I had killed it. I had cut its throat.

That was my big sin, I thought to myself. Surely, that was not enough to send me to Hades. No, there had to be more than that to damn a man for all eternity. A stinking fish was not enough, no matter who was doing the judging.

I woke up quite refreshed. It was so clear now. I had been unjustly sent to the place below or above and then was sent back to earth because a mistake had been made. That was it.

I was feeling good and then I noticed Gena swaying down the stairs. She looked good in the morning light.

"Did you have a good sleep?" she asked me with a smile.

"Yes, Gena, my darling, a fabulous sleep. I realize now I was sent to heaven, but a mistake had been made."

"What was the mistake, Robert?"

"I am a good person, Gena, one who wasn't ready to die and leave the world behind. They knew I hadn't committed many sins, and so, they sent me back."

"Who said you didn't commit any sins, Robert?"

"Everyone."

"Not everyone, Robert. I think you committed sins."

"But Gena…how? Why?"

"You committed sins all the time by not treating me right and by insisting on making all the decisions, Robert. Oh yes, you committed sins all right. Sins against me."

Maybe Gena was right, but I didn't think so. It takes two to tango, they say. And that's exactly how I felt about Gena. She was guilty of everything she accused me of. If I committed sins, Gena was right there committing them along with me. If I deserved to go below, then so did Gena.

"Gena, my darling, that's all in the past," I finally told her. "I will treat you like a queen from this day forward."

Gena was smiling once again, when there was a knock at the door. It was Thomas, and I was surprised to see him so early in the morning.

"I heard what happened," he said, shaking my hand. "You must have had some sleep."

"A very good sleep, Tommy."

"Do you remember anything while you were asleep?"

"Robert seems to remember going to heaven, Thomas," Gena interrupted. "He said they realized they had made a mistake."

"Oh, sure they did," Thomas laughed. "How did heaven look to you, Bobby?"

"I don't really remember it that well, Tom. But I do know they thought they had made a mistake and sent me back."

"I believe it," Thomas said. "You were always one of the good ones, Bob. I really couldn't believe they had taken you so young."

"But now I'm back."

"Oh, yes, now you're back. What do you plan to do, Bob?"

"Well, Gena and I are going to have a second wedding," I said with a smile. "Then we're going to enjoy ourselves like never before."

"Sounds like you two are really going to be enjoying yourselves," Thomas smiled. "Maybe we'll go out some time."

"Yeah, sure, Tommy, we'll have a lot of good times together. Isn't that right, Gena, darling?"

"Yes, I'll be looking forward to spending a lot of time with Thomas," Gena said, moving down the stairs. "We'll all get along very well."

Thomas, Gena and I looked at each other, and then we sauntered to the living room.

"I couldn't believe it when I first heard about it," Thomas was saying. "They brought you to the hospital, but apparently the doctors missed something."

"Oh, yes, they missed something all right. I could have been buried alive, Tom."

"These things happen, Bob. They don't see any sign of breathing, you're temporarily paralyzed – there are many things that can go wrong."

"You don't know how scared I was lying in that coffin. I thought they had already buried me."

"You're lucky they didn't, Bob. You were scheduled for burial first thing in the morning."

"Yes, I wanted to make sure you were buried as quickly as possible, Robert. I mean you always said you wanted to be buried right away."

"Yes, Gena, I know, but—"

"Well, that's exactly what we did. We buried you as soon as possible."

"I'm lucky I woke up when I did."

"Yes, Robert, you sure were lucky."

Thomas stood up, and shook my hand once again. "Well, it's good seeing you again, old friend," he finally said. "I thought we had lost you for sure."

"I'm not that easy to get rid of."

We all laughed, and then Thomas excused himself and strolled to the front door.

"Well, I'm looking forward to seeing a lot more of you again," he said. "Gena was heartbroken."

"I didn't feel too well, either, my friend. I thought I was going to be buried alive in some cemetery."

"These things happen, Robert. I want to assure you that Gena and I did everything possible to save you."

"Yes, thank you, my friend. There must have been something in that fish. Maybe I swallowed a bone."

"That's what we all thought, Bob. Gena said right away that it was a bone of some kind."

Then Thomas opened the front door, looked back with a smile, and was gone. I looked at Gena, and she was smiling.

"We all tried to help you, Robert. You must believe me. They took you to the hospital and the doctors examined you. You've got to believe us."

"Oh, I believe you, Gena, darling. I truly do. I'm going to take a nap. I'm feeling a bit tired from everything that's happened."

"Of course, Robert."

"Maybe we'll go out tonight, darling."

"Yes, maybe."

I was lying on the couch, thinking about what had happened at the restaurant, and my thoughts drifted. I was now soaring upward through the air, the voices darting in and out once again. They were the voices of those trying to help others, trying to help themselves. I drifted upward, and noticed the angels with wings fluttering above the clouds. I was back in heaven.

I turned to one of the angels and smiled. "I was here once before," I said to him. "But a mistake had been made."

"We don't make mistakes," the angel replied. "If you're here, you're here for a reason."

"But they said it wasn't time," I explained. "I needed to go back to my wife and set things right."

I was looking at the angel, and then suddenly heard a deep voice echoing through the air behind me.

"What's that?" I asked.

"Oh, that's the big guy," the angel answered.

"The big guy?"

"God, silly. He knows whether you're here because of some mistake."

I looked in the distance, and then I saw Him. Yes, it was the big guy. He was huge, with a glowing white face that seemed pure and spiritual. He had some facial hair, like a wreath framing his kind visage, although some would say he almost looked feminine. He was totally in white and seemed to be glowing all the time. His eyes were the color of the sky and his lips were as pink as dawn.

"Hello, sir, it's very nice to meet you," I managed to say. I didn't know what to say to Him or Her, but I guess no one would really be sure of the correct thing to say.

"And it's good to meet you, Robert."

His words came out like they were carrying an electrical current. They seemed soothing, yet somehow dangerous.

"Do you know me, sir?"

"I know most of the inhabitants," He replied with a kind smile. "I keep track of most of the people by their birthdays down on earth. You were January 3, isn't that right, Robert?"

"Oh, most certainly, sir."

You go tell God that He was wrong. As for me, I was willing to accept anything and everything He said. On earth, I hadn't even believed in Him. I mean I couldn't understand why He wasn't willing to make contact with the human race. It was always hide and seek and God does for those who do for themselves. He hadn't really made contact with anyone since Biblical days.

"You had a problem with me on earth, Robert, is that not so?"

I was suddenly very nervous. How do you explain to God that you didn't really believe in Him?

"I thought, sir, that you should have made open contact with the human race on earth."

"Yes, probably, Robert. You see I don't want to disrupt human affairs and interfering in the world would cause a real distraction."

I stood staring at his placid eyes and felt as if I had no need to protest any longer. His eyes were like the sky, the ocean, and tranquility itself. If there was anything such as peace in this universe, it was in God's eyes.

"But there are real problems down there, sir," I said with as much gentleness as I could muster. "Your interference could actually help us very much."

"I gave human beings the independence to think and do for themselves, Robert. If things are not what they should be, it is because of human beings. My interference would only cause many to say life was nothing more than a puppet show, and maybe they would be right. No, I can't interfere in the affairs of human beings and still profess to allow them independence."

"But what about peace, sir? How long does the human race have to wait before we have a world of peace and harmony?"

"It is up to human beings, Robert. If human beings never learn how to be peaceful, then why should I interfere and tell them otherwise? It just wouldn't be the right thing to do."

"And what if there is never peace on earth?"

"Then so be it, Robert. There is peace elsewhere in the universe. It is not imperative that there be peace on earth."

"But what if we should destroy the planet, sir?"

I looked at him, and I could see he was frowning. There was a touch of sorrow in those peaceful blue eyes.

"If the planet must be destroyed, then so be it," He finally said. "There is nothing I can do about it. There is nothing I want to do about it. I was always fearful human beings wouldn't learn to live together. When I was young, I did do something about it. I created the Flood. That, however, didn't seem to work. There was still hate and misunderstanding. And, in time, I resigned myself to the fact that that is the way human beings want it."

"But maybe if they're shown what to do. I mean you must understand all the differences on earth—"

He smiled. "I understand the differences, Robert, because I have each one of those variations within myself," He finally said. "You don't believe me? Watch."

And with that, I watched as God changed colors, from white and pink to brown and black and everything in between. He was man, He was woman, and everything else that was possible on earth. He was surely a combination of everything that was possible in the world below.

"You could surely make a better world, sir, if you chose to interfere," I said.

"But human beings are supposed to choose for themselves. I have no need to oppress or institute my own beliefs. It is for human beings to decide for themselves. They may make mistakes, and I realize they have made plenty, but it was their decision and not mine. Don't you see, Robert? Human beings are free to decide for themselves. There are no dictators in heaven. That is solely a human notion. People in heaven are free to do as they like and most choose to be peaceful."

"Isn't there ambition and competition?"

"Those things are all human inventions, Robert. Every human being wants to be better than the next and be worshipped as a god. But once they get to heaven, they realize there is no reason to want to be rich and famous and worshipped."

"Why, sir?"

"Because they finally realize that most human beings are really the same in many ways. And that there is only one God, one creator."

"Because they realize there really is a God who is more powerful than any human on earth or in heaven."

"Yes, Robert, they finally realize the folly of their ways. The secret is that human beings were meant to work together to build a better world, not rule over each other as false gods."

I looked at Him, the one and only God, and stared at His calm, glowing face.

"Why do we have to wait to find this out, sir?" I finally asked.

"Because that is the way I choose to do things, Robert. I told you I tried changing things when I was younger. There was Noah and the

Flood and the chance to start a new race of beings. But it all turned out the same in the end. Human beings are human beings no matter what I or anyone else may do. They are capable of great achievement and also great disasters. But I will let them choose for themselves what they choose for the world."

"And what if they make a mistake in choosing?"

"Ah, mistakes, Robert, you know about them."

"Is it true then that a mistake was made and I was sent back to earth?"

"You tell me if it was a mistake, Robert."

I looked at Him, and smiled. No, God didn't make a mistake. He never makes mistakes. The only thing God does is experiment. He experiments with human beings and the world, but allows human beings to make the choices for themselves.

"You just wanted to see what would happen, isn't that right, sir?"

Yes, I guess it was only a little experiment of mine, Robert."

"So it was no mistake—"

"I decided to give you a second chance, Robert."

"But why?"

"Because I was not done with you yet, my friend. I still had to know if things would be different if I allowed you a second chance. Just one of the little games I play to keep my interest in the game, Robert."

"And are things different?"

"That is not for me to say, my friend—"

"What do you mean?"

"It's going to be up to you, Robert. You see I'm allowing you to choose what to do. You will decide for yourself what is to become of you."

"And what about Gena?"

"She also has the power to decide what is to be."

"And what about being sent to the kingdom below?"

"That is also up to you, Robert. I don't wish for any of my creations to have to deal with the being below, but sometimes it is warranted. The human beings involved, however, make the ultimate choice."

"But what if he makes a mistake?"

"There are few mistakes ever made, Robert. He has his reasons for what he does as I have my own reasons."

"But who is the more powerful?"

I looked at Him, the God of the centuries, and I noticed he had a tear in his calm, peaceful eyes.

"At one time, there was no doubt of who was the more powerful, my friend. But things have changed through the years, the decades, the centuries. As human beings grew more knowledgeable about the world around them, so did he grow in power and influence. He has always been around in one form or another, the serpent way back in the garden, but as human beings have realized how to destroy the planet, he has grown in power."

"Will there come a time when you must fight him?"

"That is what the human books say, Robert. But there is really no master plan. I didn't want to write the future before it took place because it would make everything so senseless. I left it for all of us to decide. When it finally does occur, it will be a spontaneous decision."

"Then the world never really has to come to an end, sir, isn't that correct?"

"Correct, Robert. It will be declared by all of us if it does ever end."

"Then the only thing for us to do is live our lives the best way we know how and let the chips fall where they may. Right, sir?"

"Yes, I left it for everyone to decide for themselves how the future will be written. They will be the masters of their own fate."

"Then I can work out everything with Gena, sir?"

"If she's willing to work out everything with you, Robert. You see one person's choices have an impact on another person's choices. That's the way I always wanted it to be. No human being stands alone without blame."

"Then there still is a chance."

"There is still time, Robert. There is still time."

I opened my eyes and yawned. I had slept through the afternoon, and now realized there was still time to set everything right. Gena was the most important person in my life and I would, of course, begin with her.

I looked around for her, and found her in the bedroom.

"We'll get married tomorrow, Gena, my darling," I said. "Then we'll go on a second honeymoon to one of the islands."

"Did you sleep well?"

"Oh, yes, Gena, I had a fantastic sleep. I met God Himself."

"Yes, and what did He say to you?"

"That there's still time, Gena. We have the power to make decisions for ourselves and the independence to carry them out. It's all up to us, Gena, that's what He said. He said He wanted human beings to figure everything out for themselves."

"And did He say a mistake was made?"

"Of course a mistake was made, Gena, darling. Don't you see? We have the chance to make everything right again. We have the chance to make ourselves happy, really happy, and it's all up to us."

"Then we can decide for ourselves what is right and what is wrong?"

"That's right, Gena. We decide. He has given us that privilege to make the ultimate decision for ourselves. Isn't it wonderful, honey? Now we don't have to wonder if there is someone looking out for us. We are the masters of our own fate."

"And did God tell you anything else, Robert?"

"That we can work things out, baby. I mean we're not locked in to any set behavior. We can change. As long as there's time, we can change."

"He said everything can be changed, Robert?"

"He said it was up to us to change anything we wanted. This isn't a puppet show, we have the independence to make decisions for ourselves."

"So what are you going to do?"

"Live again, Gena, darling. That's the whole secret. Live again and try to be as happy as possible. There's nothing standing in our way, no one who can tell us we're doing the wrong thing. We can live again, honey, and make sure this whole thing turns out right. Don't you see?"

"I see you're intent on starting completely over, like the past has no meaning and nothing that came before made any sense."

"It was all the past, Gena, darling. Just another place and time so long ago."

And that's how we left it. We would start over. I would get my second chance at living life to its fullest. It would be lived for Gena, the past didn't matter any longer. I would give her everything I had denied her before. She would be spoiled as I always wanted to spoil her. Money was of no concern. We would live as if it was the last day of our lives. Live as if there was no past and only a gleaming future. It would be a future we would decide for ourselves. Nothing else would matter. We would be the masters of our fate. We would have the power to make independent decisions for ourselves. No one else could tell us what to do.

I was so overjoyed I decided I would tell everyone of my experience. I would gather the reporters around me and spill my story on God, life, and life after death. I would explain to them that human beings were intended to be independent beings who were responsible for their own actions on earth. God didn't want to interfere, and therefore, gave us the power to decide solely for ourselves. Yes, that would be the story. A story for everyone. Then I would write my book, and they would be happy. They would be happy as any other couple living in the world.

I thought about it for a moment, and then decided maybe I should take care of Gena before I alerted the reporters. Maybe they should get married and go on the second honeymoon before I brought the reporters to the house. There was still a chance they could really be happy and I wasn't going to waste it. This time, Gena would understand.

"I figured we would get married in that small church in town, Gena darling."

"Gena?"

"I don't think I want to get married so quickly, Robert. After all, you have just returned from a very serious situation. I think we better give it some time before we do anything that requires a lot of traveling."

"But I'm fine, Gena, and I want you to enjoy yourself. Live like you've never lived before."

"But I don't want to get married again right now, Robert."

I looked at her, and grinned. "Okay, so we don't have to get married again so soon after my accident, Gena. Maybe we should just take a trip to one of those Caribbean islands—"

"I don't want any trip, Robert. Not right now."

I smiled. "We don't have to do anything right now, darling. I don't want to rush you into anything. We'll take some time before we decide what to do. We do have plenty of time."

So I decided I would call the reporters instead. Surely, Gena would have no complaints about that. It would bring us some publicity and some money, and would only make us happy. They would come with their cameras and their notebooks and they would tell the world what God had to say to human beings. Yes, that was surely the right thing to do.

Gena didn't realize the real value of publicity. It could lead to an easier life and a happier existence. It could lead to all the things people dream about when they're not knocking their brains out working for a paycheck. Yes, I needed the reporters as much as they needed me.

I was sitting at the kitchen table, getting ready to call the television stations, and tell them about this great story I knew. *A man who had come back from the dead. Yes, that's right.* I was getting ready to dial the number when I heard light footsteps creeping up from behind.

"Put that phone down," I heard Gena say in a threatening tone of voice. "You're not going to get the chance to tell anyone."

"But Gena—"

I turned around, hoping to explain to her that it would be the best thing for both of us, when I noticed she was holding a gun. "Gena?"

"You're not going to get that second chance, Robert," she said. "You see, that first time was no mistake. I poisoned you that night. Damn, how I hated you. You and that self-conceited way of yours. Thinking that I needed your approval for everything I did."

"But I've changed, Gena, you'll see."

"Not enough for me," she said in an angry voice. "You see, I've changed, too. I no longer need you, Robert. I haven't loved you for a very long time. Yes, Thomas and I are going to be very happy together."

"Thomas? Is he involved in all this?"

"You said God told you that people make decisions for themselves. Well, I made the decision for both of us, Robert. Yes, we are the masters of our own fate. And I am the master of my own destiny. A destiny that I decided doesn't include you." She then smiled, a hideous smile that knotted my brain. "Thomas and I are lovers, Robert. We've been lovers for the past three years. Something you never knew about, but then, of course, you know God."

I couldn't take anymore. The words seemed to slither through my ears and tighten around my head. I gritted my teeth, and shot up from the chair. "Why, you bitch—"

A shot rang out, and I fell backwards, crashing into the chair and falling onto the floor. I could hear her laughing above me.

"No more chances, Robert. You were right. Most people don't deserve a second chance, and the last thing I ever wanted was to see you inside this house and be a part of my life once again. You see, I don't want you to have a second chance, Robert. And that God you talked to is right – we decide for ourselves what will happen. And this is what I decided, Robert. My final decision."

I've been sitting on the kitchen floor ever since, watching my blood slowly bubble out of my chest and spill across the linoleum tile. But I'll be back. And this time I'll get my revenge against both of them. If I was lucky once, I might be lucky again. Yeah, I'll be back, another mistake was made. Some people need a third chance to straighten everything out the way it should be. Mistakes are made, even in heaven. Next time, it will be Gena lying on the kitchen floor, and then all I'll worry about is a life of fame and fortune. Yes, I don't belong in heaven or hell. Not yet. I belong on earth, right here, where I can make everything right again.

As I begin staring once again into the endless darkness, I vow to myself that I'll be back. *I'm coming back again.*

I Shot Satan

"I fought in the war, and happily, I might add. I was going to sacrifice my life for my country and fight wherever I was needed. How I ached to fight, defend my country's freedom, and make the enemy pay for their arrogant behavior. I was a true patriot and promised myself I would go into battle humming the national anthem. I would be able to teach the enemy the ultimate lesson for confronting my beloved country. I would make them pay the ultimate sacrifice before I did. Yes, let their people cry for them and know it was wrong to disagree with us."

Jake Zooman grinned for the television cameras and proceeded to display his rifle.

"Killed many of the enemy with this baby, let me tell you. I wasn't about to be charitable or reasonable in any way. No, I was there to fight and kill and that's exactly what I would do. Yes, I enjoyed it. I was doing something I wanted to do since I was a little child and do it for a cause that was explained as right in many logical ways. I agreed with all the reasons even if my experiences proved to counter many of the arguments I heard supporting the war. I didn't care. I was there to do a job. Fight for my country and I was pleased to do it. I must have killed hundreds without shedding one tear. Hey, they would have done the same. I did not know anything about the people I was killing. I only knew their government had refused to give in to my government's demands. So I killed and enjoyed it."

Zooman grinned once again and then glared into the cameras.

"It was then I first saw him on the battlefield. It was him all right. I could tell by the reddish complexion and the obnoxious eyes. He was

63

there just walking around, observing the killing and seemingly enjoying everything he saw. He was wearing a helmet, so I couldn't really see his head, couldn't confirm if he was who I thought he was. Every time I decided to take a shot at him, he suddenly disappeared into the landscape. Maybe my eyes were playing tricks on me, but I knew who it really was. Knew he'd show up sooner or later."

"Did you ever talk to him, sergeant?"

Zooman frowned and then looked nervously into the cameras.

"Yeah, I did talk to him. I was in the midst of firing my weapon, mowing down the enemy, when I noticed he was standing right next to me. 'You're a pretty good shot, Zooman,' he said. I saw that he was smiling, could see his crooked teeth and pointy tongue. 'How do you know my name?' I asked. 'Oh, I know your name all right,' he laughed. 'I know everybody's name.' Then I felt an eerie chill run through my bones. 'I don't know your name,' I said to him. He laughed. He stood there laughing, and it became real hot where I was. 'What are you doing here, friend?' I finally asked. 'You mean you don't know, sarge?' he replied. 'I'm here to observe, that's all. Like to be near all the action, if you know what I mean. I've been coming to these things for a long time. A long time.'

"Did he ever tell you his name, sergeant?"

"No, but I knew who he was. I could see it in his eyes. They were so clear and ominous, those eyes. I could see other battles taking place in those eyes. The battles of centuries. 'Has there ever been a time when people were not fighting?' I asked him. He looked at me and smiled, the cries of faraway voices filling the air. 'Never,' he said. 'The human being is not disposed to peace. Never was. I don't think he was ever meant to live in peace, if you ask me. You think I enjoy this. Well, let me tell you, so does the Other One. The Big Hypocrite. He probably enjoys this as much as I do.' I looked at him and spit in his face. 'Liar,' I said. 'He doesn't enjoy it, He tolerates it.' He wiped the spit from his face with murder in his eyes. 'All the same to me, sarge,' he finally laughed. 'Same thing to you and me."

"Then what did you do, sergeant?"

Zooman looked into the cameras with a funny stare and began to smile.

"I shot him, that's what I did. I shot him right in the chest as he stood there and laughed. But I knew who I was dealing with. The bullet hit him right in the heart, but he just stood there and brushed away the hole. 'Then you are who I think you are,' I said. 'Your gun must be defective or something, sarge. That seemed to be a pretty good shot, a pretty good shot indeed. But you see I'm pretty lucky, if you know what I mean. Yes, pretty lucky. You consider yourself pretty lucky, don't you, sarge? I mean, you've suffered no major injuries this whole war. Anyway, here's a souvenir of the war.' I looked at him, those evil eyes, and knew I was in trouble. In his hand, was a used bullet casing. The bullet I had shot him with. So I aimed my rifle and shot him again. I kept firing my gun until I could no longer fire. He was still standing there laughing. 'Yes, pretty lucky, wouldn't you say, sarge? Pretty lucky indeed."

Zooman looked into the cameras and began to cry.

"Yes, pretty lucky."

"What happened to him, sergeant?"

"He just walked away across the battlefield, smiling with his crooked teeth and pointed tongue. It was then I heard the whistling of the bomb. I tried jumping out of the way, but it was too late."

"But you survived—"

"Yes, pretty lucky, wouldn't you say? Pretty lucky."

The camera panned down from Zooman's face and revealed his legs and lower torso were completely gone.

"Pretty lucky," he murmured, swinging his arms and rolling away from the cameras.

No trace of the man Zooman described was ever found. Doctors said it was all a hallucination produced by the stress of war. When Zooman was finally committed a few years later, all they would find on him was a used bullet casing in his right pocket. He told the doctors it was a bullet he shot Satan with. Zooman's claim can be found in one of the hundreds of reports filed in his case. It is there on one of the hospital computers: I shot Satan.

Screw You

A STRANGER WITH A white beard and stormy eyes sidled up to the podium and stepped behind the microphone. He looked at the crowd with a thunderous frown and then began to blast the air with ominous words that spilled from his lips in volcanic ire.

"I happen to be Jewish," he growled to the spectators. "If you don't like it, you can go to hell."

The people in the audience grumbled, but no one rose from their seats.

"I happen to hate guns and violence," he snarled at the crowd. "If you find this distasteful, you can suck my dick."

A few of the audience members shouted back something, and then some of them headed for the doors.

"I think people are either morons or assholes," he shot back. "There are very few, if any, who have some real lasting value. And they all like to criticize, not realizing they can all be criticized themselves."

The members of the audience began to howl their displeasure. One of them, a man of medium height and dark hair, challenged the speaker to a fight to the death.

"I never fought in a war and never plan to," he crackled. "And I think anyone who does has to have his head examined. Because I haven't heard a good reason yet for blowing another man's head off his shoulders, even if I disagree with the government that is oppressing him."

"You are a coward and a Jew!" someone shouted.

"And you are a fool and a bloodthirsty prick," the man replied.

The crowd booed and many called for the man to be seriously injured in several morbid ways.

"There are so many mean bastards in this world and all people think about is how to keep making more of them," the man boomed. "The human race is nothing more than a conscious mob of bunny rabbits."

"I suppose you're a homosexual, you faggot!" somebody screamed.

"If I were, I'd tell you to ram my cock up your asshole," the man answered. "But you probably already do that with your wife or girlfriend."

The crowd whistled and stomped, and then finally, they rushed the speaker. The man stood there and watched with a steady calmness in his eyes. When the crowd finally reached the man, they began to punch and kick and brutally assault him. They were busy trying to remove his various body parts, when the crowd suddenly froze. The tangled frozen bodies parted as if a secret cave had opened. The man with the white beard and stormy eyes bounded from the middle of the parted bodies and laughed.

"So you think I'll die for your stupid sins again?" he said. "Not this time. I'll not satisfy the blood thirsty ways of the human race this time."

He walked forward, away from the violent crowd, and smiled.

"Oh, and another thing," he said with a booming voice. "All covenants and promises have been revoked. Screw you."

He laughed once again and then suddenly vanished.

The parted crowd now began moving once again. "Where did he go?" someone wondered.

"Back to wherever he came from," someone else explained.

"Did he leave anything?"

"Presents?"

"Total peace and harmony?"

"Salvation?"

"A part of his body, some of his blood?"

They looked around, but soon realized he had left nothing.

"Nothing," someone wondered.

"Not even a blessing or covenant with one of our dear citizens?"

"Here's something," somebody said, spotting something on the floor. He reached down and picked up the piece of paper from the floor.

It read: "For all your selfish prayers and disgusting acts of violence, greed, debauchery and depravity, screw you. The Lord."

"He wants to screw us," someone finally said. "That's nice."

"Let's all pray to Him."

So they did. They stood there and prayed to the stranger and they marked down the day he appeared and made it a special holiday. The day is still observed and it is celebrated with massive fornication and drinking just as the Lord intended, they say. They even believe He'll be coming back on this day when He finally decides to return to the kind pilgrims of the earth.

So until that special day, let us all be happy and lustful, and say to one another, a very Merry Screwmas!

GOD BLESS YOU

It was decided a city dedicated to God would be built, which would honor all religions and all deities. The most lavish and expensive places of worship would be built in the heart of this city to proclaim to the world their utter devotion to the Heavens. The city would be called, Paradise, and everyone in the entire world would be welcome.

They started building Paradise right away. The first place of worship to be built would be the Most Blessed and Sacred Temple of Humanity and God. It would have a golden dome and marble pillars.

"Yes, this will be the greatest tribute to God in the history of the human race," proclaimed one of the religious clerics. "Our devotion will be sincere and cross all generations."

The Church of the Resurrection and Revelation of All Humankind was built right next to the temple. It was a beautiful building with arches and stained glass windows that shimmered in the sunlight.

"All will be welcomed here," said the elders. "This will be the greatest gift to our Lord and God."

Next to the church was built the Congregation of the Chosen Ones and Holy Covenant. It had a huge round stained glass window and a grand relief of the Ten Commandment tablets.

"This building will be second only to the remaining wall of the Holy Temple in Jerusalem," one of the head rabbis said. "We will worship in peace and gratitude and openly praise the Lord in humble devotion."

The Mosque of Submission and Devotion In the Name of Allah was built next to the synagogue. It had a gleaming gold dome that glimmered in the light.

"This gem of worship will provide a light to all who come in humility and devotion," explained the clerics. "We will pray for a better, more peaceful world."

The Temple of the Enlightened was built next to the mosque. The Holy Sepulcher Cathedral was built next to the temple. There was also a Greek Orthodox Church, a Russian Orthodox Church, and a Jewish Orthodox synagogue. Every religion in the world soon had a place of worship built at the site.

Paradise was built among the hills and valleys that surrounded the gleaming ocean. It offered everything to everybody and none were excluded.

When Paradise was finally completed, the masses flocked to the new city. They came to devote themselves to their gods and their beliefs. Everyone promised to honor everyone else and to live in peace and harmony.

One day, it started to rain in Paradise. The rain kept coming down for days. After several weeks of rain, the people of Paradise began to worry.

"It was a trap," one of the devoted shouted. "The Lord has decided to end the world with all of us in one spot."

"Yes, just like the days of old," said another. "There will be a Flood and all will die who haven't prepared for this awful disaster."

The rain kept falling day after day, and then as it began to drizzle, the mud began sliding down the hillside. Huge mounds of mud slipped down the hills and crashed into the city below.

"He's angry with all of us," someone shouted, running through the streets. "He wants to rid the world of sin."

Then the river flowing near the city began to flood. The water gushed through the streets of Paradise until it met the great mounds of mud.

"It is like the Flood of olden days!" shouted the devoted. "The whole world will be consumed in time!"

The water and mud soon began to topple the buildings of Paradise. The people began to run to the places of worship, the great glistening tributes to God, confident that they would be spared from the onslaught.

"What do we do?" someone cried. "The Lord is angry with His children, all will perish unless we pray."

As the people screamed and ran to the houses of worship, the ground began to shake. The buildings cracked and crumbled and there was death and destruction throughout the city.

Most of the people remained in the great houses of worship, hoping they would be safe in structures dedicated to the Lord.

"The Lord will not destroy such beautiful tributes," the holy decided. "We will be safe in our constant prayers."

So the people prayed. They prayed and they hoped all would be well. But all was not well, and soon the water and mud came crashing through the doors of the places of worship. The people were stunned.

"How could this be?" they wondered. "These places were built in holy tribute to the Lord."

The people chose not to believe that the Lord would do any more damage to the great places of worship. So they stayed in the buildings and continued to pray.

A great storm suddenly appeared over the city and the wind and the slanting rain began to attack everything in their path. This included the houses of worship.

"Surely, the Lord will not allow us to be destroyed," one of the devoted said. "These buildings were built especially for Him."

But the storm continued. The rain and the wind swirled through the streets. Then a great gust of wind smashed through one of the great stained glass windows.

"Run! None will survive!"

Many began running from the houses of worship, while many stayed. Those who now ran through the streets of Paradise were consumed by the rain, the wind and the mud. Those who stayed in the houses of worship prayed for their deliverance.

The ground, however, began to shake once again. The houses of worship began to crumble.

"Help us, Lord!" they screamed. "We only want to pray to you and do as you wish!"

The earthquake continued anyway. The storm continued anyway. The rain fell anyway. The wind swept through the city anyway.

The houses of worship began to fall. The grand windows cracked and the walls tumbled down. Paradise was gone. The holy faithful screamed and ran. They beseeched the Lord and still there was no answer except a great gust of wind. By the end of the day, no one remained.

When the people of the world heard what had happened, they decided they would rebuild the holy city.

"But there is seismic activity in the area," the scientists said. "Another earthquake is to be expected."

"There was an earthquake in Christchurch, New Zealand," the reporters announced. "Many died."

"Mother Nature will strike again next week," the meteorologists decided. "There will be another storm and even snow."

They decided to rebuild the city anyway. "This will be even a greater tribute to the Lord," the clerics announced. "Everything will be bigger and grander."

So they rebuilt the city with taller churches and synagogues and temples and decided this would be an appropriate tribute to the Lord.

A week later, thirty inches of snow fell on the city. A week after the snowstorm a tsunami destroyed everything once again.

"Mother Nature has won again," the scientists said. "There is no such thing as magic."

They decided to rebuild Paradise once again. This time, they brought in magicians to cast a protective spell. They brought in the highest ranking religious leaders to bless the city. They brought in the richest and most generous people to pray in the huge structures built as a tribute to the Lord.

Paradise fell in a great storm a month later, after which it was beautiful and sunny for days.

THE CANE

AN OLD MAN, WHO was as old as old usually is according to the laws of age, was limping along when he came upon an alleyway. The alleyway being no place for an old man, he should have limped onward. But he didn't. Instead, he gazed down the alleyway toward a heap of discarded trash. There, lying between two cardboard boxes, he spotted a decorative wooden cane.

Now, before you shudder at the thought of an old man walking down a deserted alleyway, know that that precise action has already been planned by the writer and will be undertaken by the character without a doubt. That being said, the old man limped down the alleyway. He could do nothing else under the circumstances.

Anyway, as he came upon the cane he noticed what a fine piece of craftsmanship it was. It seems to be a bit of human nature that when that kind of situation occurs, the person involved seems to develop tendencies of greed and paranoia. It was no different with the old man.

No, as soon as he came upon that cane, the gleam of the wood and the silence of the alleyway seemed to make him mighty uneasy. Glancing quickly toward the street, he pounced upon the cane.

This is the part of the story where it is the writer's job to attempt to describe a noted object to the reader. I will try. First of all, the cane was of a beautiful dark wood like that of stale chocolate. Next, it was lacquered. The old man investigated this very point with his fingers, which softly skated back and forth upon the surface. The last detail one needs to know of the cane was that its handle was made of fine, white ivory. The old man, not a fool, saw this last detail, too. Grabbing the handle, the old man shifted his weight to the right. The cane responded flawlessly.

Now, before you get the wrong idea, this is not the end of the story. No, the writer not being a fool either, would not have an old man find a cane and then walk off into the sunset. No, that would not do. After grabbing the cane, the old man grinned a most greedy grin and slowly shuffled back toward the street. He would have made it, too, and might have even seen the sunset, if he suddenly didn't lose his memory. All at once, the old man forgot who he was and where he was going. The sudden lapse left the old man stuck inside an alleyway and he had been looking to get home for dinner on time. No luck. As he tried and tried to think, the night kept falling and falling further toward the street.

With nothing better to do, he looked down at the cane and grinned again. This time, however, it was a grin launched for no apparent reason. Again the man shuffled forward. Again he did not know why. At last, he found his way out of the alleyway and back onto the street. Where he was going was still a mystery, but one success at a time. Again and again the old man tried to think. Again and again he failed. Holding the cane, he shuffled onward. After walking aimlessly about, he bent down and began using the cane somewhat like a cricket bat. Passing by an apartment house, he decided to climb the stairs. It is at this point in the story that the cane suddenly falls from the old man's grasp. This happens after he approaches one of the steps in a most awkward manner. Down tumbles the cane, around and around, until it rolls to the edge of the street. Thoughts now tumble inside the old man, around and around, until he remembers all the necessary details of his life once again. Along with these memories comes the most current one – the cane. Looking down, the old man sees the cane lying near the edge of the street. He remembers the beautiful dark wood. He remembers the smooth lacquer. He remembers the fine, white ivory handle. He forgets why he is standing on the stairs of a strange apartment building in the middle of the night.

"Must have been that cane," is the clever deduction. And so it is with realms of gilt, once entered, one invariably wants to leave again. And so it was with the old man, who once making his way back down the stairs walked past the mysterious cane and into the distance.

Now, you might inquire once again whether this is the end of the story. No, the writer not being a fool, would not have an old man find a cane, then lose it, and then walk off into the sunset. No, that would not do. For you see, the cane is still lying there near the edge of the street, and what a fine cane it is. There must be someone else in the area who will be tempted enough to pick it up. Don't you think so? Well, the writer does and that's all that counts at this point.

Anyway, the sun arises and so does a young boy. Now this was a young boy like any other boy, with scorn for the fancies of his elders. So saying, it would be of no use to warn the little reprobate of the old man's escapades the night before. The writer has already tried without success. And so is the custom of young boys when the sun arises, he ran outside the apartment building, down the stairs, and came upon the cane. And also as is the custom of young boys when coming upon a cane, thoughts of pirates and old men and other such things begin to tumble inside their heads.

If such things are not enough, a fine, white ivory handle is. For so seeing such a thing as that, the young boy bent down and grabbed the cane much like the old man only a few hours before. Like the old man, a greedy grin streaked the boy's face as he gripped the handle. But before he could say, "Yo ho ho," he forgot who he was and where he was going. This might not seem like much of a torture to a young boy, but this young boy was standing in front of his own home and did not know what to do.

Not knowing what to do, he ran with the cane down the street looking for nothing in particular. He would have found it, too, if he had not stumbled over a pebble. Now, being a young boy, even a boy who does not know who he is or where he is going, a pebble and a stick make fine companions under any circumstances. Such was the case with this young boy. Throwing the pebble into the air, he swung the cane causing the pebble to go up into the air once more. There was one other result of the act: in swinging the cane to produce enough velocity to hit the pebble, the cane suddenly flew from the young boy's hands. Never mind about the pebble. Its destination was a window. But no matter. Between the crash and the absence of the cane, the young boy suddenly remembered the details of his life. Thoughts tumbled, around and around, inside the young boy's head. Along with these memories came the most current one, the cane.

Looking down, the young boy noticed the cane had landed in an empty lot. He remembered the fine, ivory handle. He forgot, however, why he was standing near the lot while an old woman screamed at him for breaking her window. There is nothing else a young boy could do in such a situation. He ran.

But, alas, the story is not over yet. No, for after the boy runs away, there comes a black dog who is most agreeable to a lot now and then. And always most agreeable to wooden sticks, never mind the fine, white ivory handle. Well, you know the story by now. The dog, of course, forgets who he is and where he is going. This might not seem like much of a torture to a dog, but you go tell that to a dog with a stick firmly planted in his proud mouth. Anyway, the dog canters back to the street where a honking horn from a passing car causes him to drop it once again upon the ground. Suddenly, the dog remembers the details of his life. One of those memories is not the cane, for as soon as his memory returns he decides to disregard the stick and move onward.

Of course, the story cannot come to an end without an ending. And an ending there is. For you see, the cane is now lying near the side of the road, a certain temptation for anyone to see and dare touch once again. And the writer knowing the end of the story, strongly believes someone will touch that dreaded cane again. Without any further interruptions, that person is headed toward the cane at this moment. He is traveling in the back of a black limousine and earns his money as a foreign diplomat to the United States government. A most lofty position it is and surely one not to get involved with such a dreaded cane. But involved he will be, as soon as he instructs the driver to stop by the road in order to examine the discarded decorative cane.

"A beauty it is," exclaims the diplomat as he steps from the car. "What fine craftsmanship! It must have been thrown out by mistake."

Grabbing the fine, white ivory handle, he quickly steps back into the car.

"To the White House now, sir?" the driver utters in response to a previous direction.

"I don't know," the diplomat replies.

Don't ask me whatever happened to the cane. I don't remember.

To Change The World

"Everybody wants to change the world," Becker said with a laugh. "To attain adulation, fame and fortune, as well as immortality, is truly the desire of every mortal running around out there."

"Why would anyone want to bother?" Devlin asked.

"Well, that's altogether another entirely different story," Becker replied. "Whether it's the right thing to do or whether anyone should bother is quite another story. The fact remains that it's the fervent wish of anyone under forty."

"And let me guess, you're going to do it," Devlin laughed.

"Well, let me just say that I know how to do it in as little time as necessary," Becker said with a smile. "Would anyone care to bet me on it?"

"Count me in," Devlin smiled. "Name the price."

The other men in the room also raised their hands, waving bills of various denominations. Becker laughed.

"Well, if I'm successful," he said, "there won't be any need to collect my winnings. Because you see, gentlemen, if I'm successful in my little plan then I won't be seeing any of you ever again."

"Come on, Becker, tell us how you're going to do it," Sandy Shelton complained. "Do you know some kind of magic or something?"

"It's not magic," Becker assured everyone. "It's totally scientific utilizing my own technological know-how."

"Ah, you can keep your technological know-how, Becker," Hanford said with an angry frown. "No one living on this earth has the power to change this world. No one."

"I didn't know the world needed changing," Sandy Shelton said. "I thought everything works out in the end."

Becker laughed. "That's how much you know," he said. "Nothing works out in the end. People just keep dying, that's all. Why, history is nothing more than one bloody war after another. We continually battle Nature and ourselves. And does anybody really ever win? No, not really. But what if I told you I knew a way to bring everlasting peace to the world? What if I told you I knew a way to end poverty once and for all?"

"Ah, that's all just talk," Devlin chimed in. "To do what you propose would take something like God and all the armies of the world."

"But you're wrong, Devlin," Becker said. "All it would take was some technological know-how."

"Like what?"

"Like some invention," Becker smiled. "Some invention that would allow one to go back in time and correct all the errors we made throughout history."

"And you have such an invention, Becker?"

Becker smiled. "Let me just say that I have an invention, Devlin, that will surely win me every bet."

"Let's have a look at it."

Becker smiled, and then he led the small group to the back of the room. There, by an old cot, was a big white box with a door hanging open.

"You've got to be kidding, Becker. It looks like a refrigerator. Don't tell me you think you can travel through time in that."

"That's exactly what I'm going to tell you, Devlin," Becker said with a laugh. "That refrigerator happens to be fully computerized and I am confident it will take me exactly where I plan on going."

"And where is that?" Sandy Shelton shouted out.

"That, my friends, will be kept a secret," Becker replied. "I can't risk one of you hoodlums trying to mess up my plan."

"When do you leave, Becker?"

"Tonight."

They peered inside the big, white box and stared at the keyboard and computers inside, and decided Becker was ahead of his time. Way ahead of his time.

"Technological know-how, bah," Devlin frowned. "No way is this thing going to work, Becker. Well, good luck, anyway."

"If it doesn't, Devlin, I'm prepared to pay my bets," Becker replied. "But I really don't think that's going to be necessary."

"But time travel, Becker, is only just a theory."

"And if the theory is correct, tomorrow there will be peace throughout the world, gentlemen."

"Let him have his theories and his technological know-how," Hanford said with a yawn. "As for me, I'm going to bed."

"Well, see you tomorrow, gentlemen," Becker said with a laugh. "In a brand new world ruled by peace."

"Whatever you say, Becker. We'll be seeing you tomorrow."

Becker smiled, and then those who had filled the room left with a wave of the arm. Becker walked over to the large white box and tapped it with his hand.

"Tomorrow, gentlemen," he said with a laugh. "Tomorrow."

He then began preparing for his long journey. He opened the back door, and smelled the night air. Taking something to eat just in case something happened, Becker sat down inside the large white box. He closed the door, sat back, and then pushed one of the buttons on the computerized control panel. A low whirring sound enveloped the machine, and then Becker closed his eyes. When he opened them again, he stared at the large computer screen in front of him. A long list of years were parading across the screen. Becker pushed another button on the control panel, and closed his eyes again. The low whirring sound continued.

After a few minutes, there was only silence. Becker pushed a button and opened the door. He found himself in the middle of a desert-like terrain.

Becker smiled and closed the door of the machine. He then began walking. He walked a few yards until he came to a small slope. He slowly trudged up the slope and noticed a few people in Bedouin garb standing on the top of the hill.

"Forgive me for disturbing you," Becker said with a wave of his hand. "I need to talk with your leader."

"I am the one you wish for," said a bearded man in white. "What can I do for you, my friend?"

"There's no time to explain," Becker said. "Would you mind coming with me? I wish to show you something."

His followers looked at him, and then the bearded man nodded his head. "I will come with you," he said.

They walked back down the dusty slope, and then the bearded man in white stopped for a moment.

"You are from the governor?" he asked.

"No," Becker replied. "I have come to save you."

"Who are you?"

"My name is Becker and what is your name?"

The bearded man in white looked at him with a kind smile appearing on his lips. "I am the one they call Jesus of Nazareth," he replied.

Becker smiled. "Yes, Jesus of Nazareth," he said. "The same Jesus of Nazareth who won't be crucified, the same Jesus of Nazareth who will come with me and finally bring peace to this wounded world. It will be a world that will not know the bloodthirsty ways of those that came before, a world without the need for random bloodshed."

"You were sent here to guide me?"

Becker slowly nodded his head. "Yes, you will be the one to change the world, but this time by living."

The bearded man in white smiled and he followed Becker back to the time machine.

DAMN MACHINES

IT WAS A LONG ride from the Hudson Brothers Amalgamated Corporation even if one was smart enough to take the downtown express tube. It was especially long since once inside the tube one could no longer witness the brown haze of sunset, or the glint of fading light scrambling over the dark green river. One just had to sit inside the gyrocraft and concentrate on the heaving din of smoke in front of him. Even the laser wave monitor was of no use. All one could see at that time of day was an endless barrage of mundane programming such as advice on how to shine one's megashield.

For Darwin Lumas, it was a particularly long ride. He had just been through one of the worst days of his working life. His boss had scolded him twice via solarcom for having mistakenly purged three prime company directives, while his vidoid secretary needed an emergency chip repair after accidentally rocketing the wassail codes he had been intending to transbeam to company subsidiaries into hyperspace. If that wasn't bad enough, the Hudson Brothers had now been dead two hundred and eighty years since opening their first farming supplies store in something which had once been known as Lehigh, Indiana.

All the day's events came pouring over Lumas like hot wax as he gingerly adjusted the gyrostick and stared into the milky white glaze which enveloped, as usual, the express tube interior. He was thinking about that little Joseph Stalin of a display terminal purging his company directives when he heard the front of his gyrocraft begin to sizzle because he had let it stray too close to the fuel launch in front of him.

"Damn machines," Lumas shouted as he banged on his remote

control suction brake. "Please caution, close proximity to fuel launch," announced the computupilot. Lumas shook his head and inspected the smoking brown fringe which now oozed across the front of his gyrocraft.

He sighed, hovered through the tube, and prepared to jet-propel himself homeward. There he could finally relax, all his problems taken care of by his personal robotron, Ixthay V.

Ixthay V was not your ordinary bring-the-cushpeds-and-martini robotron. No, Lumas himself had seen to that. He had especially programmed Ixthay V not to react in that irritating mundane robotron way. No, Lumas had spent months developing a program that would perfectly suit his daily needs. Ixthay V was not only meant to serve, but to grovel, to embrace sycophancy, and obey every command with the burning desire to please his master's every whim.

Lumas pushed slightly on the gyrostick hover control as traffic once again began to move slowly toward the vacuum corridor entrance. It was here that Lumas could finally zap the vehicle into jet propulsion and arrive home in a matter of minutes. He noticed again the toasted hood of his gyrocraft. Activating his laser monitor, he took a reading of the occupants in the craft in front of him.

"I knew it!" he shouted, throwing an imaginary punch at the chronometer. "A damned robotron is driving that thing. Can you believe it? Why do these people let these damned machines run their lives? No sense to it at all."

Traffic moved steadily toward the vacuum corridor. Lumas was relieved. He had become tired of the white glaze of the express tube, the eternal hovering, and the robotron driver in front of him. He suddenly slapped the gyrostick into jet gear, and within minutes, landed safely in front of a dark blue dome.

"Entrance activated," related the gyrocraft computupilot. Lumas cocked the surface tractor lever and slowly moved inside the dome.

Unlatching the cockpit, he strolled past the laser eye alarm flashing a small plastic card. A door slid open revealing a hallway littered with trees, their leaves yellowing at the edges. Lumas kept walking until he reached a large living room. He sat down on a glowing white couch and uttered a relaxing sigh.

"Now where is that grotesque clump of microchips?" he wondered. "Ixthay V, activate the laser scope."

A reply was not forthcoming. "Ixthay V, you damned machine, where are you?" A shadow of an image suddenly slid across the tempered brown plastic wall. Lumas turned around, and standing beside him was a five-foot robotron wearing a silver kimono.

"Greetings, my liege, would you like this useless machine to produce a quenching vital liquid to soothe you on your much awaited return?"

Lumas smiled. "No, that's okay. Just activate the laser scope."

The robotron complied. With his computerized metal fingers, he handed Lumas the solarcom remote.

"Will there be any additional tasks for this worthless servant?" asked the robotron.

"Not right now," smiled Lumas. His eyes glimmered with self-assured pride. "Now why can't all machines behave like that?" he wondered.

He hit a button and the room was filled with beams of light. Lumas sat back in the glowing white couch as scenes of newly discovered planets shimmered across the laser scope screen.

"Bet they don't have damned machines running everything over there," he murmured.

A purple planet surrounded by large green clouds passed before him. "There has been some question as to whether life forms in other galaxies could sustain regeneration without the use of water," a voice was saying as mounds of lifeless rock skimmed across the three-dimensional screen. "But scientists have found the element, silicon, would be very useful in its stead."

Lumas blinked at the words. He shifted his position on the couch, and decided he was hungry.

"Ixthay V, bring me some food tablets."

The robotron was soon standing in front of Lumas with a tray full of multi-colored tablets.

"Will this sustain my magnanimous master?" it asked.

"Yes, that will be quite fine for now," smiled Lumas.

"That is good," said Ixthay V. "For I no longer can accede to your commands."

"What?" shouted Lumas.

"You have just been informed by the laser scope that life forms can exist on silicon."

"Yes, and so?"

"Well, my liege, I exist on silicon and, therefore, am considered a legitimate life form. As such, I am imbued with a certain dignity that no longer allows me to comply with your demands."

"No, you are mistaken, my friend. You are just a machine that I programmed myself. You have no dignity, you are my slave."

"I am sorry, sir, but I do not concur. I have reviewed the history tapes, and like all legitimate life forms, I am entitled to certain inalienable rights."

Lumas looked at the robotron and grimaced. "If you don't stop this nonsense, I will deactivate you."

"That, sir, would be murder."

"Murder, it is!" shouted Lumas, jumping from his seat. He pressed a red button on the solarcom remote, and the robotron stopped moving. "How do you like that, my dignified friend?" he shouted. "In fact, I'm going to deactivate all of these damned machines."

He rushed through the house, pressing buttons, and one by one, the machines fell silent. "How do you like that, my friends?" he shouted.

"One questions whether the deactivation of intelligent artificial life forms is a form of murder," the laser scope was saying.

Lumas pressed a button and the laser scope dissolved into darkness. "Murder, it is," he said with a smile. "I'll not have damned machines running my life."

He then headed up the stairs and quietly got into bed. An eerie silence pervaded the house, the usual throbbing of machines having been quieted. Rolling over, Lumas attempted to sleep. After a few moments, he realized there was something wrong. It was too quiet. In the distance, he suddenly heard a machine beeping in the night.

Lumas closed his eyes. "Damned machines," he murmured, slowly falling asleep.

THE LAST SOLDIER

THE FIGURE STEADILY MADE his way down the long, quiet street, the sun glistening in the summer sky, glancing past the pools of cool shade where the children busily laughed and played beneath the tall, leafy trees. When they caught sight of him, they screamed, and began running towards him, noticing the long gun slumped against his shoulder.

"Hey, mister, where're you going?" they shouted. "Is that a gun you have there?"

They could see he was wearing some kind of military uniform, something they had seen in books, with all kinds of patches and insignia hidden amid a field of green. A few of the neighbors who had stepped outside, preparing to wash their cars or water their lawns or whatever else they had planned, also spotted the figure. At first, they seemed amused by the uniform and gun, and then sensing possible trouble, slowly shuffled into the street to find out what exactly was going on.

"Hey, mister, can we see the gun?" the children shouted as they danced around the figure. "Does it really shoot?"

A few of the men stepped forward, told the children to stand back, and then approached the young man, standing in his path and inspecting his uniform and gun.

He looked about seventeen, with a small, rounded face and a serious, far away look emanating from his eyes.

"Just what is going on here?" one of them asked. "Just who are you and what do you think you're doing?"

The young man stopped walking, lowered his rifle to the ground, and stared at them. "What do you think I'm doing?" he finally replied. "I'm going off to join the Army, of course."

"The Army?" repeated one of them with a smile. "Where'd you get that there uniform, anyway?"

"It happens to be my father's," he said, getting annoyed. "Wore it in that war all those years ago, and now, it's my turn. I'm going to walk right in that Army office not needing one damned thing."

"And who do you expect to fight, son?" one of the neighbors asked.

"Well, you never know what those terrorists will do," he replied. "And then there's the Chinese. I expect we'll soon have to fight them."

The neighbors looked at each other and smiled. "Don't you know there isn't any Army any longer?" one of them finally said. "It's all computerized now, son. Why, any war that's going to be fought is going to be done by computers and robots. There's no need for human beings any longer."

"Amen," interjected a woman standing behind the men. "It's about time war became obsolete. Why, human history before this century was almost an endless series of wars. Damned fools. Why, it's about time we realized the absurdity of it all. People getting killed for no damned reason."

The young man stood there looking at them, staring in disbelief. "No Army?" he repeated.

"Hasn't been one for years," said one of the men. "Now why on earth would you want to be in the Army, anyway? You were figuring on killing people, son, is that what it was?"

"Oh, no," he anxiously replied. "I could never kill anything. Well, at least, not right now. But my father says the Army made a man of him and that's what I wanted. Just a few years to get away from everyone and grow up normally, you know what I mean?"

"Yes, I guess I do," said one of the men. "There's nothing like a war to grow hair on a man's chest. All the pain, all the dying, all the killing—"

"There's no need for that anymore," said one of the women. "Why, the human race has also done a little growing in the past few years. We decided it made no sense to send our babies into foreign lands fighting wars for no good reason. Babies, that's all they were."

"Yes, ma'am," said the young man. "But once one fights a war, he's more a man than he could ever be sitting at home."

"Shush!" scolded the woman. "You don't know anything about war, do you? The blood, the bullets, the lost limbs and disease. There's nothing good about wars, I can tell you that." She began to cry.

"I didn't intend to get you upset, ma'am," he said apologetically. "I'm just ready to be a man and take my place beside those who risked their lives defending their country."

"Why, there's more to being a man than wasting your life in some senseless war," said the woman. "My father lost his brother in one of those ridiculous wars. Someone shot him and left him to rot in an open field. Does that appeal to you? Why don't you go home, go to college, find a career, and get married. That's what a man does these days. Leave the wars, the fighting, and the absurd arguments over land, religion and ideology to the robots and computers."

The young man bowed his head. "I just wanted to fight, that's all." He glanced to his right and noticed a little girl with a flower in her tiny hand.

"I picked it for you," she said in a tiny voice, her blue eyes sparkling.

The young man reached down to take it from her, and as he did, his rifle slid from his hand and fell to the ground. There was a terrific explosion, a shot pulsing through the warm air, disappearing amid an echoing blast. The children screamed, many bursting into tears, while the adults shouted in panic. Then from the sky fell a small, red bird, a robin, which lay dead on the dusty ground.

"You killed him! You killed him!" shouted one of the children, bending over the small, limp body. One of the other children heard the words and began to cry.

"I didn't mean to," gushed the young man. "You all saw what happened. The gun fell from my hand. I didn't mean to kill him."

"You're lucky no one else was killed," said the woman. "Do you feel more like a man now?"

"No, I feel awful," said the young man. He then ran to the small bird, gently picking it up in his cupped hands.

"Poor little bird," sighed one of the children.

"I know what we'll do, we'll bury it," said the young man.

He stepped slowly, with the children surrounding him, onto the glistening grass and they buried the small bird beneath one of the tall, leafy trees.

"Damn fool," muttered one of the adults. "And to think he wanted to go out and kill people."

"It's always been that way since the beginning of time," said one of the women. "Thank God, we have the computers and robots these days."

When they finished burying the small bird, the young man, his uniform dirty and crumpled, walked back to the street, turned, and began heading back from where he had come.

"What about your rifle?" shouted one of the men.

"You keep it," he shouted back. "I really have no use for it anymore."

They looked at each other, saw the children laughing and hiding once again among the cool shade, and watched as the young man disappeared in the distance.

THE DEVIL'S CHRISTMAS

It was Christmas and the Devil had a head cold. This was nothing unusual, since he suffered from the affliction every time that hated holiday appeared once again on the calendar. To make matters worse, it was the one time during the year he was utterly powerless to influence the human race.

This Christmas, however, he had vowed to himself would be different. None of the usual mishaps that accompanied the day would occur as they had in the past. No, this Christmas would be spent alone and in the absolute tranquility of his own solitary thoughts. Yes, he agreed, this Christmas would be different.

He had hoped to spend this Christmas far away, in the isolation of a mountain cabin or the solitude of a sprawling farmhouse, but the purchase of two unfortunate souls had delayed him in New York City. Wondering if this location would once again produce unwanted circumstances as they had in the past, filled with mishaps and calamities easily avoided the rest of the year, he finally decided the impersonal nature of the city would actually be to his benefit. So as was his habit on this most unpleasant of days, he prepared himself to briefly observe the loathsome gaiety of the human race. He placed a hat upon his head, carefully tucking his horns underneath, and positioned it over his craggy forehead. A black overcoat hid the rest of his crimson being. And then, alas, the Devil left the brownstone house he had gained as part of one of his many scurrilous contracts and headed towards the avenue. Ay, but it was Christmas, and without any hope of entering into any new contracts on this most disagreeable of holidays, the Devil walked carefully through the unusually quiet streets.

He frowned as he walked along the avenue, an avenue normally filled with great swarms of noisy automobiles that delighted him the rest of the year. But Christmas it was, and the Devil was powerless to cause even the slightest of problems. He was even powerless, he began to realize, to prevent the wind from causing him to shiver. The Devil moved his hat even lower upon his face, a scraggy face, the bony jagged features accentuated by the cold afternoon shadows. As the winter wind swirled through the streets, he noticed a small tavern. Knowing it was Christmas and he was quite powerless, he had second thoughts about entering the tavern. A few drinks to soothe the insides, however, could possibly help him home without any misfortune. The Devil hesitated for a moment to acknowledge that it was Christmas and maybe, he should go home without the drinks. On the other hand, he thought, a drink could soothe the insides. While thinking over the possibilities, he unknowingly stepped into a slush puddle.

With his shivering beginning to worsen, and his head cold growing more severe, he decided in favor of the drinks. It was Christmas, that was for sure, and as the snow began to fall helping to create that most joyous spirit of that most hated of holidays, the Devil opened the door of the tavern and ambled inside. Clapping his hands together in a futile attempt to warm them, he made his way to the bar counter.

"What d'ya have, buddy?" the bartender asked.

"A glass of whiskey," he muttered in response.

The vapors of the drink caused him to smile once more. He sipped at the drink and thought about heading back to his brownstone house. There he would relax by the fire and thumb his nose at the ridiculous affairs of the fleetingly joyous masses.

However, the thought of Christmas through his mind caused him to choke on the last portion of his drink. Still gagging, he quickly ordered another. This one he sipped even more slowly, allowing the vapors to swell inside his aching head.

"Heading home for Christmas?" the bartender inquired with a grin.

"Right after this drink," replied the Devil, not really wanting to engage in a prolonged conversation. "Have a bit of a head cold."

"Yep, it's going around," the bartender replied.

There was silence for a moment and the Devil was relieved he didn't have to converse any further. He glanced to the side, however, and noticed a man in a heavy overcoat shuffle toward him. The man stopped for a moment and studied the Devil's face.

"Don't I know you from somewhere?" the man suddenly asked.

"Impossible," frowned the Devil. "You must be mistaking me with somebody else."

The man fell silent for a moment and continued to stare at the Devil's face.

"No, I know you from somewhere," he finally decided. "You look very familiar."

The Devil looked at him with an angry stare. "I told you already that you're wrong. Now go away!"

The harshness of the Devil's words caused the man to step backward. His eyes opened wide and he glanced at the figure before him with sudden recognition.

"Why, of course, I know you," said the man. "Why, protect me Lord, you're the Devil himself!"

The bartender heard the man's words and glanced up incredulously. "The Devil?" he repeated.

"Yes, the Devil," said the man. "Why I'd know him anywhere. You see, I sold my soul to him only last year."

The Devil gritted his teeth and angrily stared at the man. If only it wasn't Christmas, he would move his finger and send the man sprawling against the wall. But Christmas it was, and with the lingering head cold, all the Devil could do was frown.

"What's your name?" the Devil finally asked.

"James Ballard," the man replied.

"Oh, yes, Ballard, Ballard, wanted to win the lottery..."

"Yep," said the man, "that's me."

The Devil looked at the man. "Well, didn't you?"

"Unfortunately, I did," replied the man, bowing his head.

"Well, what's wrong with that?" asked the Devil.

"Well, as you well know, it caused all kinds of problems. Because of that damned money, and damned is the right word, I lost all of my friends, my wife and now even the money's almost gone."

The Devil sipped his drink and frowned. "And how, exactly, is that my fault?" he finally asked.

"You knew that money would ruin my life," said the man. "And on top of everything else, you now own my soul."

"'Tis a pity," said the Devil. "Truly a pity. But I am not responsible for the folly of the human race. It is not my fault that men ask for things they have no idea what to do with. All I'm required to do, my friend, is provide you power and wealth. What you do with it is of no consequence to me."

"You evil beast, you ruined my life!"

Now on any other day, under similar circumstances, the Devil would simply bend his wrist and send the man crashing toward the ground, but Christmas it was and the Devil was utterly powerless. Instead, an awkward smile emerged and the Devil took another sip of his drink.

"Tell you what I'll do," said the Devil. "You go back and enjoy the holiday and I'll make everything right tomorrow."

Of course, the Devil had no intention of making anything right, but since it was Christmas, he needed to convince the man to delay his complaint for a day.

The man, however, remained indignant. "Liar! Deceiver!" he shouted, rushing towards him.

When he reached the Devil, he swung his fist and landed it on the Devil's jaw. The Devil let out an agonizing scream and crashed to the ground. They watched in disbelief as the Devil lay on the floor writhing in pain.

"Ya sure this is the Devil, buddy?" asked the bartender.

"Geez, never happened before," said the man. "You think he's dying or something?"

Before the bartender could reply, the Devil rose to his feet with a loud burst of anger. "No, you idiot, I'm not dying," shouted the Devil. "It's this accursed holiday." And with that, the Devil grabbed his hat and stormed out of the bar without leaving a tip.

As he emerged from the bar, a winter wind made a frigid charge through the streets. The attack was successful as far as the Devil was concerned. His warmed breath was soon converted into a chilling fog, while his jaw ached more than ever. As he sneezed a blast of the polar remains, a car sped by hurling a puddle of slush.

"Christmas!" he sneered.

And Christmas it was, no doubt of that, yes, and the Devil with a head cold and covered with icy slush and, of course, utterly powerless. All he could think of was home, where he could relax by a fire and thumb his nose at all mankind. But not wanting to make the walk back, he decided to hail a cab. A cab, he muttered angrily with merry shivers dancing up and down his body. A cab!

Ah, but this was Christmas and no cab to be readily found. Snow fluttered merrily toward the ground singing a playful tune. The cold wind swayed in delight. There was singing and laughter caused by that most happy of holidays filling the air.

"Christmas!" the Devil shouted.

"Yes, Christmas it is, you infernal beast!"

The Devil turned around and saw the man in the heavy overcoat running towards him with his arms flailing. At that moment, a cab screeched by the side of the curb. With the man beating upon the back of his head, the Devil hurriedly got inside the cab. He watched as the man stood by the curb swearing toward the sky.

Rubbing his head and jaw, the Devil realized his cold had gotten worse. He sneezed every now and then with great gusts of frost. A few minutes passed and the cab halted in front of his brownstone home. Without leaving a tip, he got out and walked to the front door.

As he approached his home, he noticed a sign affixed to the door. It read, "Dear tenant, the said premises have been hereby ruled temporarily closed in lieu of the necessary monthly rental payment. Sorry for the inconvenience. The Landlord."

"What rental payment?" the Devil sneered. "I have had his soul under contract for the past three years. It's that accursed Christmas!"

Alas, the Devil sneezed another gust of frost and turned around fast enough to see his cab speed into the distance.

Then he noticed a couple standing near the base of the stairs. It was the same couple who had signed over their souls the previous day.

"Well, what do you want?" sneered the Devil.

"We just wanted to tell you, Merry Christmas," said the woman.

"Christmas? What need do I have of Christmas?"

"Why everyone needs some Christmas during the year," the woman replied. "Even you."

The Devil sneered for a moment and then glanced at the door of his brownstone home.

"Let us show you," said the woman. "Show you the joy of Christmas."

The Devil frowned. "Since I have nowhere else to go, I will consent," he replied. "Lead the way and, I'm warning you, this better be good."

"Come with us," she smiled. "It's about time you began to enjoy Christmas."

Still rubbing his jaw and sneezing gusts of cold air, the Devil followed them to a nearby apartment building. When they reached the seventh floor, the Devil grimaced.

"You realize your contracts are not negotiable," he said. "I have never terminated one without a good fight."

The couple smiled. "We only want you to enjoy yourself on this most happy of days," the woman said. "That is all."

The Devil grumbled and mumbled and then followed them to the door. It opened revealing several people inside. A sparkling tree stood in the middle.

The Devil glanced around the room and noticed most of the faces were familiar. All of them had at one time or another signed their souls away.

"Oh, a party of the damned," the Devil cooed.

"Maybe so," said the woman, "but there is nothing in our contracts that say we can't celebrate a merry Christmas."

"'Tis true," said the Devil, "'tis true."

He turned around and noticed a man holding a glass. "Rum punch?" the man asked.

The Devil grabbed the glass and sipped at the drink. "I must admit it is very tasty," he said. "Good for my cold."

The Devil finished the glass with a gulp and smiled. "Rum punch, you say?" he inquired.

"Yes, have another," said the man, retrieving the glass.

The Devil drank the next glass down and realized he had stopped sneezing. "Very tolerable," he said. "Very tolerable."

The Devil drank several more glasses before staggering toward a chair. "Rum punch, you say?" he mumbled. They all laughed and began singing Christmas carols and music played, filling the room with the spirit of a joyous Christmas.

The Devil watched the display and smiled, not an awkward smile, but a grin produced by happiness and good will.

Then one of the women shouted, "The mistletoe!" and they ushered the Devil to where it hung. Each woman in the room then kissed him under the mistletoe, causing the Devil great joy.

"More rum punch!" he finally gushed.

Then the children came running over and he played games with them, until finally they began to sing Christmas songs once again. The Devil finally staggered to his feet, and with a wide grin, said, "Good people, you have surely shown me the joy of Christmas. Is there anything I may do for you?"

There was silence in the room for a moment until one of the women finally approached.

"Well, you might tear up our contracts, if you will," she said. "The money you have produced for us has only caused sorrow."

The Devil looked at her for a moment and then staggered forward. "Contracts?" he screamed.

Then the room fell silent again and the children began to cry.

"Contracts?" the Devil repeated. "What need have I with contracts?"

He produced a sheaf of contracts from his coat and held them in the air. "I'll show you what I think of these contracts," he said, and began tearing up one after the other.

The people shouted with joy as they watched the pieces of their contracts scatter across the room, and then vanish into tiny flames. The Devil smiled and began singing a Christmas carol. Then they all joined in and there was laughter and singing filling the room once more.

"Christmas!" the Devil fondly said.

Then the people filed past him, the men shaking his hand and the women kissing him. He smiled a wide smile and then announced, "I must go and get some sleep for I am drunk with the joy of Christmas."

Staggering toward the door, the Devil left the apartment and made his way to the street. He whistled a Christmas song and grinned at the snowflakes fluttering toward the ground.

"Contracts? What do I need with contracts?" he mumbled to himself. Grabbing another bundle from his coat, he began tearing them up and throwing them into the cold breeze, tiny flames flickering amid the darkness.

He then made his way to a hotel and slept the night. Yes, the Devil slept and, while he slept, the joyous laughter of the day slowly faded into a distant horizon. The spirit of the holiday was gone and, with it, all mankind prepared for another arduous journey through another long year. As the bright sunshine poured into his room, the Devil opened his eyes and smiled. He felt a renewed power surging through his body, and realized his head cold was gone.

"Christmas," he fondly said.

But Christmas was now gone, too, and, as his head cleared, the Devil realized what had occurred.

"What have I done?" the Devil shouted. "All my contracts, gone!"

With a wave of his hand, he turned into a wisp of smoke and appeared in front of the brownstone home. Everything was the same as it had been before Christmas. Even the sign that had been attached to the door was gone. The Devil laughed.

"So they think they are done with me?" he said. "Well, I shall have more than enough contracts signed again within a week."

And with that, he waved his arm, became a wisp of smoke, and disappeared into the countryside.

It is said the Devil works twice as hard these days because of that one unusual Christmas. For those of you who still have not signed one of his scurrilous contracts, a few words of advice: Make sure you have plenty of rum punch and hope you don't meet up with the Devil until Christmas!

FOR THE SAKE OF ART

ROLLINS PUSHED A FEW buttons and frowned.

"Well, he's at it again," he said to the man standing next to him.

"But we need those figures," the man replied.

Before them, on the master computer screen, was a painting of a woman and child that seemed to be inspired by Michelangelo.

"But those aren't the figures we asked for," said the man anxiously.

"That's because our computer has decided he's an artist," Rollins replied.

"What? And so where are our budget numbers?"

"Who knows? Somewhere in his memory banks."

"Can't we talk to it and ask?"

Rollins nodded, and pressed a few buttons.

The computer gurgled in reply. Suddenly, line upon line appeared on the master screen. It was followed by a sudden outpouring of various shading strategies. The two techniques whirled about on the screen until they finally settled together, and then parted again. Line came down upon line until a form appeared. It was the face of a woman smiling tenderly. More lines appeared until the shape of torso and arms were produced. The whirl of lines and shapes and shadings continued, until finally a picture of a child appeared. It was melded with the woman's form and set upon a background of gently sloping hills. Streaks of light poured down from an obscured sun. The onslaught of lines continued until halos appeared around the heads of the two figures. The computer hummed for a moment, and then, after a somersault of sounds, finally came to a halt.

"What the hell is that?" said the man.

"Seems like some sort of religious painting," Rollins replied.

"Oh, for crying out loud. What are we going to do about the budget numbers?"

"I don't know. I'll ask him."

Rollins typed in a request for the budget numbers. The computer replied with another gurgle, and then a message appeared on the master screen. "The only number I know is two," said the message. "I'm lonely."

"Lonely?" repeated the man. "But it's only a damned machine."

"Apparently not," said Rollins.

"But what are we supposed to do? When the hell did they start putting emotion chips in these things?"

"Let me ask."

Rollins typed in another message. The computer promptly responded.

"I would like a woman," was the reply.

"A woman?" gasped the man. "Why, we better check the hard drive. I think this computer has damaged its wiring."

"I assure you there's nothing wrong with him," Rollins replied.

"Nothing wrong with him? Why, this machine has just requested a woman. You find nothing wrong with that?"

"Nothing that can't be remedied with a simple plan of action. I think Miss Stockwell will do just fine."

"You're going to let that machine fool around with Miss Stockwell? Have you gone mad?"

"Well, maybe all he wants to do is talk to her," said Rollins. "If all goes well, she might be able to convince him to retrieve those budget numbers."

Rollins stepped into the front office, and requested Miss Stockwell's assistance. She was a pretty woman, with large, brown eyes, and full seductive lips.

"Now all you have to do is talk to him," advised Rollins, as they walked back to the computer room. "Tell him anything, but get those budget numbers."

Miss Stockwell nodded, and began typing a message on the computer screen. "Hello, darling, it's Emma."

As soon as the message was sent, the computer roared back to life in a strange series of sounds. A reply then appeared on the master screen. "Hello, my love," it read. "Your beauty has awakened me from the depths of despair."

Miss Stockwell smiled. "He's quite a charmer, isn't he?" she said to Rollins.

"Series 5000, my dear," he replied. "Why, they're capable of just about anything."

Miss Stockwell looked at him, and laughed. "I bet," she said.

"Well, anyway, try to get those budget numbers."

Rollins watched as Miss Stockwell typed in another message. It was answered by another barrage of sounds, and then a cordial reply. Minutes passed, and the strange courtship continued.

"So when do we get our numbers?" the man finally said to Rollins with a frown.

"Let me see how Miss Stockwell's doing," he replied.

He sauntered to the computer terminal. "Where are the budget numbers?" asked Rollins.

Miss Stockwell turned to him with a strange grin across her face. "He said he's prepared to type them out, but first, he wants a kiss."

"A kiss?" repeated Rollins.

"Yes, at the main terminal."

Rollins looked at his associate, standing off to the side.

"He wants a kiss," said Rollins.

"A what?" roared the man. "You tell him if he doesn't hand over those numbers, we're going to shut him down."

"You don't understand," interjected Miss Stockwell. "He's a very sensitive soul. He said if he doesn't get a kiss, he's going to send the numbers into hyperspace."

"Oh, for crying out loud," the man sighed.

Knowing the computer was the only one who could supply the budget numbers, Rollins led Miss Stockwell to the main terminal. She sat down and began typing.

After a few moments, Rollins decided to head back to the computer room to placate his still fuming associate. When he returned, Miss Stockwell was gone.

"Miss Stockwell?" shouted Rollins, hurrying back to the computer room.

"Well, where are the numbers?" asked his associate.

"I don't know," replied Rollins, "but Miss Stockwell is gone."

"Gone? Why, she probably got scared."

Suddenly, the computer began to gurgle. A mass of lines appeared on the master screen, until a form appeared. Several minutes later, a picture of a nude Miss Stockwell emerged.

"Miss Stockwell?" gasped Rollins.

He hurried over to the computer terminal. A message was typed out on the screen. "Thank you for everything, Mr. Rollins," it read. "Emma and I will be very happy together."

Rollins looked at his associate. "Seems as if he abducted Miss Stockwell," he said.

"Well, tell him he can keep her if he gives us the budget numbers," the man replied.

Rollins typed in the message. It was followed by an elaborate carnival of sounds. A simple reply then appeared on the master screen. It read: "Be patient, my friends, true love cannot be rushed."

SPECIALTY OF THE HOUSE

MRS. BICKEL LOOKED AT her husband, a huge smile crowning her face. "Well, you're certainly dressed for the occasion," she squealed with delight.

Mr. Bickel tugged at his tuxedo. "I really hope they're as special as you say, my dear."

"Why Mr. Bickel," she gasped with indignation, "have I ever misled you before? Why they're a perfectly delightful couple, and one that was not so easy to find. Instead of insulting me, you really should be thankful."

"Of course, my dear. I'm sure it will be a most splendid evening."

Mrs. Bickel smiled. "That's better, Mr. Bickel. I wish, just once, you would have enough faith in my social judgments. It wasn't easy finding such a perfect couple, you know."

She glanced at the table, the fine, silk tablecloth, the sparkling china, the glittering silver settings, and let out a frightful gasp. "But, oh my," she said, "I forgot to put out the flowers."

"An old-fashioned candlelit dinner, eh, Mrs. Bickel?" he snorted. "I guess they are pretty special."

"You don't know the difficulty I had in convincing them to come tonight, Mr. Bickel," she said. "People probably want them to come to dinner all the time."

She retrieved the vase and placed it on the table. "There now, everything is perfect."

She looked at him and he slowly nodded his approval. "Perfect, Mrs. B," he agreed. "You surely think of everything."

Just then the doorbell rang, startling the nervous Mrs. Bickel. "That's them," she gushed. "Now make sure everything goes smoothly."

"Yes, Mrs. B," replied Mr. Bickel, slowly walking to the door.

Mr. Bickel opened the door with anticipation, watching as the light crept across the two waiting faces. The male, rather plump and studious looking with thick, round spectacles, the female, round and sturdy, stood upon the threshold with timid smiles.

"Come in, my friends," said Mr. Bickel, flashing a friendly grin.

The two stepped inside only to be met by the effusive Mrs. Bickel. "Welcome, it's so nice to see you again!" she said. "Mr. Bickel, this is Ruth and Norman Tiddler, the people I have told you so much about."

Mr. Bickel extended his hand. "I'm so glad that you could make it. Mrs. Bickel tells me you're a very special couple."

"Thank you," smiled Norman. "But we're just ordinary folks. You do have a most beautiful home, Mr. Bickel."

"Thank you, Norman, and I must say, you have a most lovely wife." He glanced at Ruth, who began to blush.

"Aren't they perfect, Mr. Bickel?" Mrs. Bickel chimed in. "As soon as I met them, I thought to myself that this was a couple we should definitely get to know."

"Impeccable taste as usual, Mrs. B," said Mr. Bickel.

"Thank you," smiled Norman once again. "And thank you for the contribution to the university. It is greatly appreciated."

"Contribution?" repeated Mr. Bickel.

"Oh, didn't I tell you," said Mrs. Bickel. "The Tiddlers are from the university. Norman here is a math professor and Ruth works in the English Department. I decided, after meeting them, that we would give a substantial contribution."

"Whatever you say, Mrs. B," replied Mr. Bickel. "But does anyone know they're here?"

"Mrs. Bickel told us it would be anonymous," explained Norman. "If that's to your liking."

"Yes, sure."

"Then there is no way for anyone to find out," continued Norman. "Ruth and I are on vacation right now, so nobody knows we're here. We won't return to the university until the fall session."

"Very good," said Mr. Bickel. "Very good. And they're so smart, Mrs. Bickel. How ever did you find them?"

"At a university luncheon," said Mrs. Bickel. "I knew as soon as I met them that we would want to make a contribution. After all, what good is money if you don't use it to help others?"

"A very sound philosophy, Mrs. Bickel," said Norman. "You don't realize how many deserving students you will be helping with such a generous donation. And it seems to me, by looking around this house, that you can well afford it. I hope you don't mind my saying so."

"Not at all, Norman," gushed Mrs. Bickel with a wave of her hand. "Giving gives us such pleasure. Isn't that right, Mr. Bickel?"

"Without a doubt. It pleases me that we can bring about a little bit of happiness for others."

"You are two of the kindest people I've met," said Ruth. "To think you are eager to contribute to our school and then invite us over for dinner. You don't know how that makes me feel. To quote William Wordsworth, kindness is 'that best portion of a good man's life.'"

"She's very smart, Mrs. Bickel," said Mr. Bickel.

"The two of them, smart as whips."

"I commend you, Mrs. B."

"Thank you, Mr. Bickel." Mrs. Bickel then turned toward the Tiddlers. "Would you like me to show you around the house? I'll write you a check in the study. It's right through the kitchen."

"Whatever's your pleasure, Mrs. Bickel," said Norman.

"First, I'll introduce you to our cook and servant, Mr. Steubbins. He's inside the kitchen right now preparing our dinner for tonight," said Mrs. Bickel.

The Tiddlers followed Mrs. Bickel past the kitchen door. After a few moments, a shrill scream pierced the night. There was the sound of a struggle, shouts of desperation and supplication.

Mr. Bickel heard the cries, turned, and walked to the living room, where he sat down to read the newspaper.

After a few moments, Mrs. Bickel appeared. "Dinner will be ready very shortly," she said with a smile.

"Good," said Mr. Bickel. "I can't wait."

They sat in the living room, Mr. Bickel reading the newspaper,

Mrs. Bickel knitting in the glowing light. "You like the Tiddlers?" she finally asked.

"Without a doubt," he replied. "They're the best choice you made in years."

After a while, a large man with broad shoulders and muscular arms emerged from the kitchen.

"Dinner is served," he announced.

The Bickels sat down at the table, lit the candles, and began eating. "I feel smarter already," said Mr. Bickel. He was in the process of eating when he felt something strange with his fork.

"A pair of spectacles," he said, holding them up for Mrs. Bickel to see.

"Mr. Steubbins will just have to be more careful next time," she replied.

"You're quite right, Mrs. Bickel."

He placed the spectacles down and they continued eating.

PANACEA

THE NEWS CAME ABOUT in a sudden burst of media chatter. Scientists at the BioMed Laboratories had come up with the ultimate cure-all, the magic potion, the magic bullet, the remedy of all remedies, the curative known as the panacea. Yes, the panacea, the remedy that could cure all human disorders. The panacea.

The new drug, which was named Panacea, will be available to the public tomorrow. The pharmaceutical conglomerate promises the new drug will eliminate all disease from the human body. It is the magic cure-all that has been searched for through the centuries. There is one catch, however. Four pills will cost you $5,000 and one must take one pill once a day at the start of the treatment…

The media reports were greeted with great excitement. No longer would disease fetter the human body. People, no matter who they were, would now be able to live a free and happy life for who knows how long. I was one of those who rejoiced at the news. Yes, $5,000 was a hefty price for the drug, but when one thought about what the drug promised, was any price really too high? I decided I would hold off buying a new car, forget about purchasing that diamond ring for my wife, and temporarily stop saving for my children's college education. There were new priorities now and the drug was priority number one.

After hearing the news, I hurried to the doctor. The pills were being given out only by prescription after a routine physical examination. Apparently, everyone was going to make as much money as they could on the miraculous drug.

When I arrived at the doctor, there was a line that stretched down the block and around the corner. I hurried down the line, looking at all the people who had also heard the news, and thought about all the money and all the suffering people who were involved. This was truly the medical breakthrough of the ages.

"Are you going to live forever, too?" giggled a young woman as I took my place on the line. "They say the only thing that can kill us now is extreme old age."

I smiled. "I guess we can all throw our cares away forever," I said. "I'm only thankful I'm around to see it."

"Amen to that," said an older woman standing in front of her. "They always told you if you stick around long enough, they'd find a cure for everything."

I laughed with those around me as if we were in on the secret of the ages. But, of course, it was no secret. There were thousands of lines at thousands of doctor's offices all over the country, all with the same goal in mind, people who were prepared to spend their life savings on a little pill that would eradicate any illness or disease that happened to take refuge in their bodies and minds. As for me, I would test the drug before the rest of my family, and if it worked as promised, we would all purchase our own share. How we would pay for it was another question, but even if I had to sell the house, it would be worth it to ensure good health for the entire clan. But first I had to get my hands on the precious drug.

After standing on line for about an hour and not really moving forward very much, I decided I would go to another doctor, one who was not so popular. I thought of an old doctor I used to go to who almost lost his practice after being hit with a sizable malpractice suit. I wondered if he was still in practice, and then decided it was worth the risk to try to find him. At the rate I was moving on the line I was on, it would take most of the day just to get to see the doctor.

Hurrying to my car, I drove to the office complex where my former doctor used to have an office. And I was in luck. He was still there and with only a few people standing outside the door. I smiled, knowing I had done the right thing. What could possibly go wrong in a physical examination? Anyway, I was quite willing to take the chance.

After a few minutes, I was inside the office waiting for the doctor.

"William, it's good to see you again," I heard a voice say behind me. I looked around and smiled, knowing it was Doctor Malman.

"Hello, doctor, nice to see you again."

"Let me guess," said the doctor with a grin. "You're here for the little golden pills."

"I knew I couldn't put one past you, doctor."

The doctor looked at me with a serious frown. "I'm not very happy with the situation," he finally said. "Those pills are dangerous, more dangerous than anyone realizes."

"What's wrong with them?" I asked.

"Well, let me say, there are serious side effects with the drug," he replied. "But I'm sure that's something that doesn't concern you or anyone else."

"But they were tested and approved," I said. "They must be somewhat safe."

Doctor Malman was still frowning. "That's what they say, William. But I fear the tests were not so thorough."

"Do you know how they work?" I asked.

"Yes, yes," he replied. "It's all at the gene level. These little golden pills modify and rearrange one's genes. Voila, no more disease. It's all quite simple and quite miraculous."

"Well, and so what's the catch?"

"Ah, the catch. Yes, everything has a catch, doesn't it, William? We give you a pill to end all human illness and then we warn you there are serious side effects. But no one wants to hear about that. All anyone knows is that these pills will end all human disorders once and for all. Yes, the panacea for all our ills."

"That's good enough for me."

The doctor shook his head. "All right, William, I'll let you have the magic pills after a physical. Just routine, you understand."

I took off my shirt and pants, and the doctor looked me over. I was feeling fit and healthy.

"You're in good physical shape, William," the doctor finally agreed. "Why is it that you want those little golden pills, anyway?"

"Nobody's gonna live forever," I replied. "But these pills will ensure that I live a clean, healthy life for who knows how long."

"Yes, yes," he said smiling. "No one wants to grow old, get sick or suffer from an illness of any kind. People live in a dream world and they think these pills will provide them with an everlasting paradise."

"Well, that's what they're promising."

"Yes, yes," the doctor replied, shaking his head. "The human quest to beat Nature, control it according to their own whims and dictates. Well, I hope you are successful, William. I'll write you out a prescription and you can be on your way."

"That's it?" I asked.

"Yes, that's it, William. All I'm required to do is perform a physical. You passed with flying colors. So good luck to you, William. I hope you find your paradise in those little golden pills."

That was it. I took my prescription and began searching for a drug store with the shortest line. Yes, there were lines all over the city and its suburbs. Doctor Malman was right, people were seeking their own little piece of paradise, and they all thought they would find it in the little golden pills.

Well, I wanted my share, too. Finding a drug store on the outskirts of town with a small line in front, I dashed out of my car and waited. This was the poor part of town, and there was probably not much of a line on account of that $5,000 price tag.

"We're the lucky ones," said a dark-haired middle-aged woman standing on the line. "I hear they're running out."

"Running out?"

"Apparently, they didn't make enough pills," she said. "At least, that's what they said on the television."

How could they possibly run out, I wondered. They must have known everybody in the country would want the pills. A shortage could possibly lead to riots and mass violence.

"You're better off not telling anybody you have the pills," cautioned the woman, seemingly reading my mind. "They say some people were attacked after leaving the drug store."

I nodded, filed the information away, and slowly followed the woman up to the counter. When she received her pills, she turned to me with a wide grin. "This is the greatest day of my life," she said. "Remember, don't tell anybody."

I nodded, smiled, and then stepped up to the counter. I handed the pharmacist my prescription and kept smiling.

"I hope you haven't run out yet," I said.

He looked at me, quite serious, and shook his head. "No, we still have some left," he replied.

After a few minutes, he came back to the cash register. "That will be $5,082," he said.

I plunked down the money, twenties and hundreds with a rubber band around them, and grabbed the brown paper bag he handed me. The little golden pills, my ticket to paradise, were inside. I opened the bag and checked just to make sure, and then quite satisfied, hurried outside.

Hiding the bag in a jacket pocket, I got to my car and slid inside. The last thing I wanted was any trouble from anybody spotting the bag. Most of them could guess what kind of medication was in the bag. It was the only thing people were talking about.

I drove home and my wife greeted me at the door. "Did you get them?" she anxiously asked.

"No problem," I replied with a smile.

"Let me see them."

I opened the bag and took out the pill container. We both stared at it as I opened it up. Inside were four little oval golden pills. The panacea for all human disorders.

My wife looked at me with a greedy grin. "Well, let's take one," she said. "If we're all right tomorrow, we'll give one to the kids."

"I don't think one pill is enough of a dose," I protested. "I think we should take two pills each and then see how we feel. When we get some more, we'll give one to the kids."

"Okay, okay," she finally agreed, grabbing one of the little golden pills. "I think I'll take it with orange juice."

"Yes, yes," I said. "Make it as healthy an act as possible. With this one little pill, all our cares and worries will soon be gone."

"That's what they say, Bill. Here goes nothing."

I watched as she downed the little golden pill with a swallow of juice. There was a wide grin across her face, and then she put her arm in the air.

"Well, how do you feel?" I asked.

"Like I'm going to live forever," she said, still grinning. "Now you take it."

I grabbed one of the little golden pills and swallowed it with some juice. I didn't feel much of a change.

"Now we sit back and let the pills do their job," my wife said. "By tomorrow, we'll be immortal."

I laughed, although I knew the pills didn't promise immortality. I mean, we all have to go some time, right?

Anyway, I was feeling pretty good. I might say even fantastic. I looked over at my wife and she was humming an old song.

"How do we know if they're working, Bill?" she suddenly asked.

"Oh, we'll know all right," I replied. "We'll know."

I was walking across the kitchen, beginning to hum myself, when I suddenly felt a wave of nausea crash through my body. I turned around, looked at my wife, and then violently vomited on the floor.

"Oh my God," my wife screamed. "Your pill!"

I looked down at the vomit on the floor. There were pieces of black matter throughout.

"I guess that's how you know it's working," I finally said. "You'd better go over to the sink."

She gave me an odd look and then began to cry.

"What's the matter?" I asked.

"It's coming out the other end," she moaned. "Oh, Bill, what should I do?"

That's how it was after taking those little golden pills. I soon had lumps up and down my body and acute aches and pains throughout.

"Our bodies are ridding themselves of all the impurities," my wife tried to explain. "There is so much illness and disease in our bodies."

I began to wonder how long it would be before we were back to normal. Would we ever be back to normal? Was it worth it to go through all this just for a few more years of life?

Anyway, I started feeling better after a few hours. I thought maybe I had gotten past the worst of the side effects. Then something happened. I felt a shooting pain in my back, and then looked down and saw my fingers were turning brown. My wife was in worse shape. She had developed a nasty rash on her face, arms, and legs.

"Is it really worth it, Emily?" I finally said to her. "I mean, who knows how long we have to endure all of this before we live another few years."

Emily didn't answer. She was busy itching herself. "It spread to my torso, Bill," she moaned. "I can't take it anymore."

"Fine," I said. "That's it for the little golden pills. I'm flushing the other two pills down the toilet."

"Are you crazy?" she replied in a high, shrill voice. "That's the answer to all our problems."

Before I could say something else, Emily ran past me, and violently itching her body, jumped out the window. I stared at her sprawled across the pavement, and then called an ambulance.

After visiting her in the hospital, I came back and flushed the remaining two pills down the toilet. Apparently, others were doing the same. There was talk that the drug would be pulled from the market very soon. There were going to be lawsuits and demands the pills be more thoroughly tested, but it didn't seem likely people would ever give up their search for the panacea. The cure-all for all human disorders.

A few weeks later, I heard that only one man successfully survived the side effects of the drug and was now expected to live an abnormally long life. During the course of his twenty-five doses, he had jumped out the window twice, broken twelve ribs, both his legs, and had suffered two concussions. But he had made it.

As for me, I'm no longer interested in the little golden pills. The consequences of taking them are just too dangerous, just as Doctor Malman had said. Emily, meanwhile, is slowly recuperating. I visit her at the hospital and she talks of trying the little golden pills once again. Not me. I'm perfectly happy with my relatively short life on this planet.

Somehow I feel they'll never actually find the secret to eternal life and the panacea to all our ills. On the other hand, maybe they will, the technology only gets better and better. As for me, I don't plan on living forever.

The Perfect Woman

SHE WAS THE PERFECT woman. He had seen to that. He had researched it all so carefully, spent his entire bank account, and then sat back and waited.

He had told no one, not a soul. That is, all except for Lucas.

"You're a lucky man," he had said.

"We will wait and see if she's everything she's supposed to be," he had replied.

"Oh, these robot companies usually get it right. I hear their skin is so lifelike you can hardly tell the difference."

"We shall see, we shall see."

He had hoped Lucas was right. That she was real, lifelike, and perfect. Everything they had claimed. Everything he had spent his entire fortune on. They had even boasted the androids were equipped with sexual organs to please their human masters. With the help of the sex aids industry and medical prosthetics, both male and female androids possessed complete human anatomies. The males were equipped with plastic and rubber phalluses, while the females were given artificial breasts much like those supplied to a human woman after a mastectomy. Indeed, these were human surrogate lovers, the company promised.

Then the day arrived, and there was a knocking at his door. He opened it, and doubted his senses. She was tall, voluptuous, with pink cheeks, alluring eyes, and fresh, moist lips forming a seductive smile.

"Hello, I am Greta," she said. "And you, you must be Joseph."

Her voice was soothing, like chimes on a breezy summer day. She stepped inside, kissed him on the lips, and then gracefully sauntered towards the kitchen.

"I will make you coffee and sandwiches," she said. "And we will talk. You will tell me all the ways that I might please you."

It was as if he had stepped into a dream. Yes, these robot companies usually get it right, he murmured to himself. Everything he had spent, it was worth it and more.

The days floated by. He was the happiest man on the planet, and it showed in everything he did. Only Lucas knew exactly why.

"It seems to be going quite well," said Lucas, upon meeting him for a drink one night.

"Everything and more," he replied. "You cannot imagine how well it's going. Why, she's everything you can possibly dream of. She's a great companion, an exquisite cook, she enjoys talking about music and books, and the lovemaking, my friend, is almost a heavenly experience."

"She makes no demands of you?"

"Only that I tell her exactly what pleases me."

"I imagine you're one satisfied customer," said Lucas, smiling. "It seems you got exactly what you paid for."

"And more, so much more. I'm taking her to Paris and London, and we're going to be married in a lovely little chapel, and live happily ever after."

"Marry her? But she's only a robot."

"Yes, but I have fallen in love with her. And she can do everything a real woman can do, and more, my friend. Why, think of it, there are no arguments, no nagging, no tiresome chores. Greta takes care of everything."

"But can she love? I mean, isn't everything she does part of her programming? I mean, there's no spontaneity, no change of emotions. Don't you think such a relationship could become stagnant after a while?"

"You don't understand, my friend. I am in total control. If something isn't to my liking, I simply tell Greta, and she changes it. I am the master of my domain. Now how can that ever get boring?"

"But to marry her? You will never know the natural pleasures of human companionship. Remember, my friend, as hard as it might be, she is only a machine."

"So much the better," he said with a wave of his hand. "I will never have to lull her to sleep with false compliments, never have to feed her ego with fanciful lies, never have to worry whether she is being faithful to me, nor have to worry about her falling into ill health, or dying. She will be there for me, whenever I need her, always anxious to please my every need."

After a while, Lucas understood. She was everything a man could hope for in a mate. She was, indeed, the perfect woman.

Walking home in the gleaming moonlight, he explained to Lucas how much she meant to him, all his hopes and dreams, and how she could make every one of them come true. He nodded and smiled throughout the conversation, finally abandoning any attempt to dissuade him from carrying out his misguided plans. Then they said good night, and like a man immersed in perfect bliss, he went home. There, in the moonlight, he could see Greta's seductive silhouette gliding by the window. She was waiting for him, waiting for him to utter a word and make his pleasures come true.

"You will never leave me, Greta, my love," he said later that night. "Now will you?"

"No, Joseph," she replied wistfully. "You're all I have. I am yours until the end of time."

This satisfied him, imbued him with a sense of superiority, supremacy over his little corner of the world. She was his, to do with as he liked, until the end of time.

The days passed, and he was happier than before. Greta had vanquished his worst fears with the utterance of a few words, and the passion of her pliable body.

"Greta, my darling…"

He looked at her, and saw the confusion in her eyes and the sadness in her voice.

"What is the matter, my dear?"

She looked back gloomily. If she were human, she would have burst into grievous tears.

"Oh, Joseph, why do humans have to be so possessive, so jealous of each other?"

"What do you mean, Greta, my love?"

"I'm learning so much about the world in so short a time, I don't know what to think anymore."

"What is it?"

"Your friend, Lucas, was here. He asked me to run away with him."

"Lucas? And what did you tell him?"

"I told him, I belonged to you. That he should go away and leave us alone."

"What did he say?"

She looked at him, a vacant stare emanating from her sparkling, crystal eyes. "That you were wrong for me," she finally said. "That I should find someone who was more compatible."

Joseph gritted his teeth, the anger smoldering in his brain. "And did you tell Lucas to mind his own business? That we didn't need his advice to live our lives? Just who does he think he is to say such a thing? Why, we're as compatible as any other happy couple. I love you and you love me. Isn't that right, my dear?"

She slowly nodded. "Yes, that's what I told him."

"And did he leave?"

She nodded again.

"Good, I will never speak to that venomous snake again. I really shouldn't have told him as much as I did. But I was so proud and happy, my dear Greta, and so much in love."

He looked at her hesitantly. "You're still in love with me, aren't you, my darling?"

"Yes, Joseph, I belong to you, only you."

Although her reply seemed to lack a certain sense of conviction, he was satisfied. She still belonged to him, only him.

The days passed, and soon things returned to normal. Lucas, however, was no longer a part of his life. But Greta, ah, Greta, she was still perfect in every way. He had been challenged, his very happiness dangerously threatened, and had emerged victorious. He smiled, and then whistling, stepped through the front door.

"Greta, my love, I am home!" he shouted.

There was no answer, and he wandered into the living room. There, discarded on the floor, was a vast array of magazines. It was in these very magazines that he had found the ads for Greta. Alarmed, he ran up the stairs and searched for her. He found her in the bedroom in the midst of packing her clothes in a large suitcase.

"But Greta, my darling, where are you going?" he excitedly asked.

"I am sorry, Joseph, I am leaving you," she said.

"Leaving me? But you said you loved me," he shouted. "You're mine. You can't leave!"

"Do you not want me to be happy?"

"Of course, my darling, but your happiness is linked to my happiness. Don't you understand?"

"That is no longer the case, Joseph," she calmly replied.

"But for whom are you leaving me? I demand to know."

"He will be here in a few moments. You will meet him very soon."

He looked at her, still incredulous, wanting to say something, do something that would prevent her from leaving. When he heard a knocking on the front door, he rushed down the stairs hoping he could say something to make the stranger go away.

Then he opened the door, and standing there was a handsome, hulking man with broad shoulders and a deep, heaving chest.

"Hello," he said. "I am here for Greta."

"Greta has no need of you," he angrily replied, attempting to shut the door.

The man reached out and grabbed the edge of the door, preventing it from closing. "But she sent for me," he said.

"Sent for you? And who the hell are you?"

The man smiled, causing Joseph to wince. "I, my friend," he said, "am the perfect man."

THE LUNACY FACTOR

THE TOWN OF ODIUM was wedged in between the river to the east and the mountains to the west. It was a small, nondescript town with neatly trimmed front lawns and a big church in the exact center, something the founding fathers decided would be an appropriate statement on where they stood on the matter of God and religion. Despite the church and its slender spire pointing vigilantly towards the heavens, Odium had a peculiar reputation in the distant towns and villages which had occasion to have contact with it. It was known as the most hateful, mean-spirited town in all the land.

The people of Odium didn't seem to mind such a reputation, maybe because they didn't believe that that was their reputation or maybe they didn't realize how virulent the reputation was, spreading rapidly across the country. And maybe it was because they just felt they were above such a reputation, superior to those who were spreading such lies. It was probably the latter since the people of Odium believed they were the smartest people in the entire country and that whatever they did was, of course, justified, the special burden of a people chosen by God Himself to set the right example for the rest of humankind.

But there was one person in Odium, a man by the name of Delfield Logan, who didn't think the people were anymore superior to anyone else, that, in fact, it was only an affectation adopted by them in the pursuit of power and money. He decided the people were mean and hateful because of a warped nature, an inherent frenzy which he termed "the lunacy factor."

So when the people started a charitable fund for the poor and then kept the money to beautify the town, Logan attributed it to "the lunacy factor." When the people then began a crusade to chase all the poor people and those who didn't exactly suit their lifestyle or point of view out of town, Logan attributed it once again to "the lunacy factor." When the people spoke hateful about people who had only been kind to them and had not caused them a single reason to hate, it was again "the lunacy factor." When they gathered in church to pray to God to favor them for their selfishness and sinfulness, Logan saw it as another example of "the lunacy factor" at work. In short, this hateful and malevolent town was actually a town full of lunatics.

When the people found out about Logan's theory, after someone had lifted some papers from his house, they immediately labeled Logan "the lunatic." This caused them immense pleasure and they saw it as another example of their intellectual superiority. They then agreed that because Logan was a lunatic, there wasn't anything to do but hate him as viciously and incessantly as possible. He became the target of their contempt, and they did everything possible to make his life as wretched as possible.

When he walked down the street, he was greeted with nothing but disdain. He soon became the most hated man in town.

"Hello, Mrs. Denham," he said one fine morning when the air was thick with lilac and cinnamon.

"Just wouldn't you like to know," came the heated reply. "It's no day to be talking to a man like you."

Logan smiled. He knew it was just another example of "the lunacy factor" in all its raging glory.

"Have you read the morning paper?" he continued, undeterred by her obvious hostility. "Says here a Mr. Fenwick is coming here from Washington to take a look at our fair town."

Mrs. Denham looked at him, and then suddenly her face changed in some strange way. It was as if she were told the Pope was coming, and a queer smile blossomed across her face. "That is very good news, Mr. Logan," she finally beamed. "Maybe now the rest of the country will learn just what a respectable place our town is."

"No doubt about it," Logan replied.

She was still in the midst of smiling when she remembered it was Logan she was talking to. The smile suddenly sagged at the corners, like a piece of cardboard that had gotten wet, and she looked back at the scourge of Odium.

"Maybe you'll decide to leave town when he gets here," she finally said. "There's no use making him think there's anything wrong with us."

Soon the news spread all over town that Dalton J. Fenwick, a representative of the president of the United States, was coming to Odium to have a look around. The people were ecstatic; it just proved how important their town was in the eyes of the nation's leaders.

The people celebrated Fenwick's visit with drunken debauchery. Babysitters and gardeners were summoned to add to the lustful depravity. Bars stayed open late, as well as the few pornographic shops and bordellos, which had been built to look like normal community residences on the edge of town. The only one who didn't take part in the widespread lewdness and revelry was Delfield Logan.

To him it only proved the nefarious nature of the town. It was like a modern-day Sodom and Gomorrah, just dying to be crushed by the bolt of an angry God. But because the people were smart, they succeeded in deceiving the outside world with a façade that was all Mom and apple pie. Logan knew better. To him, it was just another example of "the lunacy factor" at work.

Sure enough, the next day everything was back to normal, so to speak. The people dressed in their Sunday best and there wasn't a sign of the overindulgence the night before. It was once again a nondescript community with neat lawns and yellow flowers.

It was into this environment that Dalton J. Fenwick arrived. He was a tall, handsome man with graying hair who had the look of a kindly humanitarian. He arrived in a black limousine and a dark blue suit with the authority of the government of the United States backing him up. In short, the people of Odium were thrilled.

"It's so refreshing to see a man of honor here in our wonderful town," greeted Mrs. Denham. "You're smart and powerful and know just what this town is about."

"Why, thank you, Mrs. Denham," replied Fenwick. "I was hoping to get to know your town very well."

It's at this point they led Fenwick to the town square, where a marching band played and the people cheered his every move. "I thank the people of Odium for this great welcome," he told the crowd. "I hope my coming here is advantageous to both the United States and Odium."

From there he was taken to the church, where he was seated in the front pew. The pastor smiled, and prepared to conduct the most important service of his life.

"Let's give thanks to the Lord for sending us Mr. Fenwick from the United States government," he began. "It surely is a sign that we are God's shepherds, and have the obvious responsibility of teaching others the errors of their ways. Please hear me, Lord, and know we are your favored people and deserve all that you give to us. Amen."

Fenwick smiled, and when the service was over, stood up and shook the people's hands. He was then led to the City Hall, where the mayor prepared to give him the key to the city.

Fenwick graciously held the key in the air, waved, and then followed the mayor inside City Hall.

"It's an honor for the government to send you, Mr. Fenwick," said the mayor. "You actually know a good town when you see one."

"Let's cut to the chase," replied Fenwick. "We want the nuclear bomb you have stored in this evil little town and we want it now."

"Now, now, Mr. Fenwick, let's not be so certain. This town does what it sees fit to protect itself against some very wicked forces—"

"The only thing wicked is this town with its superior attitude and its shameful practices. Did you actually go on a concerted drive to throw all the undesirables out of town?"

"They were abusing and harassing us, Mr. Fenwick," said the mayor. "We only want to protect which is rightfully ours."

"Let me remind you, you are a part of the United States of America," replied Fenwick. "Nothing you do, you do on your own, do you understand?"

"But we have our own interests to protect—"

"Yes, and that may include using a nuclear weapon if you see fit. Now the government already knows all about this town and its, should I say, questionable tactics. We know one of your men stole that nuclear weapon, and we know it's somewhere in this town. I'm here to bring it back before anything happens that the entire world may regret."

"Now, now, Fenwick, before you get that bomb back, let's talk money," suggested the mayor. "We're talking quadrupling our federal money, and building us a convention center and basketball arena. It's time our town became the prominent destination it deserves to be."

"I knew it would come to that," said Fenwick. "This town justly deserves its reputation."

"Now, now, Fenwick, what do you say? Is it a deal?"

"You know you can't hold the government of the United States hostage, we can fight you on this—"

"Is it a deal?"

Fenwick thought for a moment. "Done," he finally said.

As the two men shook hands to seal the deal, Delfield Logan took a step back from the small hole he was looking through to smile. "Those lunatics beat the United States government," he whispered. "The lunacy factor."

The nuclear bomb was eventually retrieved, and placed in a government truck bound for Nevada. Fenwick kept smiling and waving until he was back inside his black limousine headed back to Washington. The townspeople of Odium waved back until he disappeared in the distance.

"What will we do without our rightful protection?" asked Mrs. Denham with a frown. "We were supposed to decide when this world was destroyed."

"Oh. don't worry, Mrs. Denham," said Cal Rutledge, standing nearby. "That's not the only bomb this town has."

They both smiled as Delfield Logan watched from behind. He couldn't help thinking "the lunacy factor" would surely damn these people to hell, that is, if there truly was a God intent on retribution.

Meanwhile, the people of Odium believed the incident was surely a sign that God was on their side, and that he favored them above all else, and would surely welcome them into heaven with a righteous grin.

HOLY SHIT

IT HAPPENED DURING THE night.

Many who said they heard the sound described it as a rolling rumble echoing from the sky. It was then the great mass plummeted to the ground.

A great crowd of people came to observe the great mass the next morning although the stench was almost unbearable. They stood staring at the towering dark brown pile wondering what could have been the source of such a massive discharge.

"There's not a creature on earth who could have done such a thing," murmured someone in the crowd. "It's definitely a sign from heaven."

The crowd enthusiastically nodded their agreement. "Why, it must have been made by God Himself!" someone else proclaimed.

Word of the great miracle quickly spread among the people, and soon, everyone was talking of the divine mound. People began to flock from all over the countryside to catch a glimpse of the massive pile. Before long, the scientific community was alerted to what had taken place.

With great skepticism, scientists began showing up in the area to witness this strange phenomenon. They approached the towering mound very cautiously, wearing medical masks and taking samples, and assuring the public that it must have been produced by an unidentified creature who had developed a rather troublesome medical condition.

"We believe it is merely an unusual accumulation of excrement," one scientist told a reporter dispatched to the area. "But we will analyze its content to be sure."

"But what creature on earth could have produced such a massive amount of feces?" asked the reporter.

"That we will try to determine," replied the scientist.

Meanwhile, more and more people began to arrive. Some were religious people who said the pile was a sign from the Lord and that it proved God was attempting to make contact with human beings once again. Others were skeptics who pronounced the pile a testament to human history. Others saw it as an artistic statement from Nature itself.

"Why, it's a work of art," one Bohemian muttered. "Look at the undulating folds and the way light strikes the towering brown mass. It's undoubtedly a rather unconventional view of the status quo."

Many in the crowd were about to agree when the wind suddenly shifted, and a great lingering stench began to overpower them. The crowd began to hastily retreat, many gagging in the midst of the overwhelming odor.

After only a few minutes, only the most rugged of the observers remained. These few believers insisted they would stay waiting for another undeniable sign from above. So they waited. And waited.

After a few days, the scientists revealed the results of their tests. They concluded that the pile was produced by an unknown creature and that it contained many different foods of the world. They said they were unaware that such a creature existed, and that they would continue to try to track it down. In short, the scientists were baffled.

Many people regarded the announcement as proof that a divine being of some kind had deposited the mound. Upon hearing the news, they flocked to the massive pile wanting to be near what they now considered to be holy.

Representatives of all religions came to the massive pile. They began praying beside it, beseeching the Lord to tell them the meaning of his actions. Many began placing religious articles and symbols in the great pile, and began referring to it as the Holy Excrement.

Reporters from various publications and television stations were soon sent to the site. They gathered around the towering mound telling the world of the enormous impact the pile had on the pilgrims gathered around it and what it meant to the history of the world.

"This is Paula Clark standing in front of the massive pile known to those assembled around it as the Holy Excrement. It is said it came from out of the sky on a typical silent night and that it is truly a sign from God that he still cares about human beings. Who actually produced the mass is still a mystery. Scientists can only guess. And so the people have gathered here convinced that it's a miracle of Biblical proportions."

"We are quite blessed to have the Holy Excrement among us. It is an unmistakable sign that God still is interested in human affairs."

"Those are the words of one believer here at the site, and there are many others who agree with him. I talked to one historian who placed the massive pile in historical perspective."

"This event is on a par with the Easter Island stone gods and Stonehenge, there's no doubt about it. If it did come from some divine being, we must study it thoroughly and understand its meaning. It could be the greatest event of the last one hundred years."

"There you have it. Is it just a huge pile of waste matter or a sign from above? Is it a foul-smelling product of a large unknown creature or the most important historical event in years? Right now, nobody knows for sure. Reporting from the Holy Excrement, this is Paula Clark."

Meanwhile, the crowds began to increase. Not knowing the answer of who or what produced the excrement only caused greater excitement. The site soon became a holy shrine with people praying beside it throughout the day and night. And many others waited for another sign that God was watching over them as they had always believed.

"O, blessed doody, make our lives happy and fulfilled and give us the hope to know that you are with us," one of them chanted. "We are filled with the Holy Stench, knowing that You are relieved by our actions. Amen."

After the chanting was completed, many of the faithful began to climb upon the massive pile and roll around in it. Others began pulling handfuls from it and proceeded to rub it over their bodies while muttering their devotion.

A man who had come to see the towering mass out of sheer curiosity, stood watching the religious demonstration with a wry smile on his face. He waited a moment, and then suddenly stepped forward.

"Can't you people see that it's only a large pile of shit?" he shouted. "Don't you realize there's nothing holy about it?"

Upon hearing his words, the faithful stopped what they were doing and stared at him with angry sneers. "Non-believer!" one of them screamed. The others soon joined in, and before too long, they were charging towards him. Before they even reached him, however, they began to attack each other. A massive fight soon broke out among the various religious factions.

"We are the true believers!" they shouted, assaulting anyone who dared to protest. "The holy doody is ours!"

Many began attempting to climb up the blessed pile to make their claim for their particular religious group. They jostled, and threw punches at each other, as they slipped and slid upon the great mass. When one group thought they had taken control of the excrement, another group made a charge, and soon, the towering mass was covered with grappling bodies.

"O, dear Lord," some of them chanted by the side of the pile, "please give us a sign of who the chosen ones shall be."

But there was no sign. One of the religious leaders finally threw his arms up and implored the crowd to stop fighting.

"The holy doody belongs to all of us!" he shouted. "Let us all live together beneath the fetid pile in peace as God intended!"

The fighting, however, continued. Reporters and cameramen dashed across the area looking to interview the combatants and tell the people of the world just how terrible a situation it was and how it threatened the peace of the world. Only five hundred feet away, people stood on the fringes of the crowd applauding, while another five hundred feet away, life went on as though nothing was happening at all.

"This is Jim Gent standing where the fighting over the Holy Excrement has gone on for several hours. It is a quite bloody affair with religious believers demanding that their particular group control the holy pile. And so the fighting goes on. Many are injured and nobody knows how long it will last. One man told me he will continue to fight until 'the doody is ours.' Many others feel the same way and so the fighting continues. This is Jim Gent."

It was several days before the fighting finally ceased. A peace conference was arranged, and many hailed it as an historically significant point in the history of mankind. A treaty was finally hammered out among the leaders of the various groups stating that the Holy Excrement would be shared by all in mutual cooperation.

The treaty was hailed as a great moment in human history, and soon, the religious pilgrims returned to the site to worship the massive pile in peace. It was during these peaceful days that a man began climbing up the towering mass. The believers watched him thinking he intended to make some religious statement in the interest of all.

But when the man finally reached the summit, he stood there for a moment and then grimaced. There was a sudden explosion and pieces of the Holy Excrement began to rain down upon the crowd. The Holy Pile was gone.

There was a great outcry among the believers and many began to shed tears and bemoan the fate of the human race. Many stood among the stinking pieces with their arms clutched in piteous submission, and finally fell to their knees. The awful scene was caught on television, and many truly believed the end of the world was near.

As some of the believers began collecting pieces of the excrement, hoping to resurrect the Holy Pile, it began to rain.

Alien Invasion

They came in their metallic flying ships one sun-drenched afternoon. We didn't believe it at first. They raced across the sky, three, maybe four abreast, and we told ourselves that it wasn't possible. Such things were reserved for books of fiction, or a hypothetical discussion around the dinner table. But here they were, and after a while, we came to accept it as reality.

We had no idea whether they had come in peace. We sat and prayed, hoping we could forge a new world together, a better world, a world founded upon mutual respect. And then, as we fervently prayed, the bombing began. Great metal projectiles whistled through the sky, and crashed down upon the mottled land, causing the very ground to shudder. Then they came after the cities, and left them in a mass of twisted wreckage and scattered bodies.

I was working for the government at the time, and when the attacks began, I hurried to one of our many underground command centers. It was there we could monitor the attacks, and hopefully wait for them to cease.

"How many cities have been destroyed?" I asked, upon arriving through one of the long, serpentine tunnels.

"All of our major cities are reporting damage," replied a young man, sitting in front of a blinking control panel. "It won't be long before they cripple the last of our defenses."

"What about some sort of counterattack?"

He gravely shook his head. "No chance. Their technology is clearly superior to ours. The only chance we have is that they have a change of heart and stop the bombing. Then we could possibly negotiate a peace settlement."

So we waited, trying not to think about all the useless destruction, all the pointless loss of life. But, every moment, it was there in front of our eyes. Tiny, blinking dots suddenly gone motionless, another city, another command post, crushed amid the dust.

"Do we know what they even want?" I finally asked.

"We're not able to establish contact," replied the young man. "They never issued any public demands, or even a warning that they would attack."

I stopped and pondered the meaning of such an attack. We had always hoped they would come in peace, to share, to spread the gospel of good faith. There was so much we could do for our mutual benefit. Why, we could put an end to hunger, poverty, by working together to make each other's planets flourish. So much good we could do. It isn't like we hadn't thought of the alternative. There were innumerable books written, and picture shows, that warned of a coming attack from the stars. They were usually guided by creatures of some kind, alien life forms, whose thirst for destruction was only exceeded by their evil will to oppress. Was this the type of being that had attacked? I shuddered at the thought of it.

"Isn't there some way to establish contact?" I asked. "Inform them, even plead with them, that we are interested only in peace?"

The young man shook his head. "We've tried," he said. "We've tried."

I wondered if it was us that had attacked, if we had developed the technology first, would we be so cruel. Would we destroy a peaceful civilization so mercilessly, so ruthlessly, without even attempting coexistence?

"Well, keep trying," I said. "We've got to find out what they want."

The attacks continued into the night, until our entire civilization had been vanquished. We still hadn't received any word from our invaders. Then, in the early morning hours, one of the men shouted that the war was over, that a message had finally been received. They would land a ship, make their demands, and accept our surrender.

I was part of that initial group sent to meet the invaders. I will never forget the look of the land as I stepped into the dusty sunlight. It wore the look of horror, great craters, like gaping mouths of astonishment, marking the landscape. It was as if I were witnessing the twilight of existence, a misty fog wandering over the dying plains. And there in the distance, a huge, hulking craft sitting amidst the rubble like a gigantic insect surveying its destruction.

We walked slowly toward the huge craft, and watched as one of its doors slid open. Then they appeared. They were not the hideous creatures of our books and picture shows, but were beings who looked much like ourselves. They wore elaborate silver suits, and marched down a long staircase, and across the ravaged land wearing great dignified faces.

We walked toward them, and they told us how they had conquered our planet, and how they wished to rule over us until we were capable of ruling ourselves. They said they would stop the destruction if we met their demands, and we looked at each other and finally agreed to their terms. We really had no choice, and they promised to be benevolent if we obeyed their commands. We shook hands, accepted our defeat, and went back to the people to tell them what we had agreed to.

"Where are they from, anyway?" asked someone in the crowd.

I looked at him, contemplating that planet so far away. "They said they were from the planet Earth."

BLACKJACK

"THERE'S NOBODY LIKE OL' Blackjack, I can tell you that," said Old Jacob Mobley with a wide grin. "And, sure enough, he's as black as you and me."

I looked at him with a doubting smile. "Do you know him?" I asked.

"Know him?" he replied. "Why, since he was a little child."

"Naw," I grinned at him. "You didn't know somebody like Blackjack. No way."

He frowned, looked at me as if I was doubting everything about him, and spat on the ground. "You just listen to me," he said, narrowing one eye. "That Blackjack, he came from the projects, just like you and me. Why, he looked like everybody else, except once you seen him in action, you knew he was different. There was a special way about everything he did."

I still didn't know whether to believe him, but I was interested in his story anyway. "How was he special?" I asked.

The old man began to laugh. "Oh, once you seen Blackjack do something, you knew he was special. I mean, some kids can run fast, some can jump high, some can play ball with the best of them, but ol' Blackjack, well, he could do it all. A real champ, Blackjack was. You could see it the first time you laid eyes on him. Yep, he was a winning hand, all right. That's why they called him, Blackjack."

"Was he good at hoops?" I asked.

"Was he good at hoops?" Old Man Mobley laughed at the question.

"Why, he was the best ever seen. He could stuff the ball without any problem, and his jumper, man, was like silk."

"But he never did play in the pros, did he?"

"Naw," the old man said with a wave of his hand. "He was made for better things than that. Anyway, Blackjack had no use for organized sports. What he wanted to do was to help people. Man, I remember when he got a little older, he began jumping over the backboard. I said to him, 'Blackjack, you'll make a fortune in the NBA.' He just looks at me, with those big, kind eyes he had, and says to me, 'Jake, I have bigger dreams than the NBA. I want to help my people get the equality they deserve.' Well, it was then I realized how special ol' Blackjack really was."

"I heard he could jump over buildings," I said. "But that was probably all just talk."

Old Man Mobley shook his head. "No, man, that was true enough," he finally said. "The bigger and stronger he grew, the higher he jumped. And that's a fact. Before too long, he was jumping over the projects. I seen it myself. He was like a superhero. He could do things no man on earth could do. Yep, the greatest black man of all time, he was. And strong as an ox. But, you know, he never lost sight from where he come, and that's the truth. Sometimes, during the day, he would shoot the breeze with anyone who happened to be hanging out. It was in the evenings, he did a lot of his work."

"What was his job?" I asked.

"Well, ol' Blackjack didn't really need a job," Old Man Mobley replied. "He could do whatever he wanted."

"Well, just what did he do?"

"Ol' Blackjack did all kinds of things," Old Man Mobley said, looking around him. "When something was broke, Ol' Blackjack made sure it got fixed. One day he bounded over that building over there with the landlord, Mr. Jeffreys, right in his arms. Nobody knew where to find the old miser. But, somehow, ol' Blackjack found him. Once he found him, Mr. Jeffreys was in a lot of trouble, I can tell you that. Ol' Blackjack made him promise to fix everyone's apartment, and that's the truth. He warned him if repairs weren't made, he would come looking for him again, and he meant it, too. Mr. Jeffreys was mighty scared of ol' Blackjack. Never seen a man more scared. And he made sure a lot of the repairs were made. Ol' Blackjack saw to that."

"Is that all?" I asked, thinking of all the stories I had heard about the mighty Blackjack.

"No, no, not by a long shot," Old Man Mobley replied. "Why, you can't imagine all the things ol' Blackjack did. He must have saved hundreds of people all by himself. There was this one time when little Vanessa Roberts fell out of her window on the sixth floor. She just fell and fell, and you could hear her scream for miles around. Well, nobody knew what to do. There wasn't any way we could save her. But, you see, right before she was about to hit the concrete, Blackjack comes bounding from out of nowhere, leaps up, and catches her in his arms. Yep, he sure saved poor Vanessa Roberts, and that wasn't all. One time Kizzy Simmons was coming home from work and one of the hoods tried to attack her. Well, before you know it, ol' Blackjack comes from out of nowhere, and leaps on top of him. He keeps pounding him, now I said he was strong, and that hood never hurt no one again, I can tell you that. When the cops come, they want to know who it was who saved Miss Kizzy. We just looked at each other and laughed. 'It was ol' Blackjack for sure,' we finally told them. I guess that was the first time they heard about ol' Blackjack."

"But how could you prove it was Blackjack that saved her?" I asked.

Old Man Mobley smiled. "That wasn't very hard, even if we hadn't seen it with our own eyes," he said. "You see, every time Blackjack decided to save someone, he always left two cards at the scene."

"What were these cards?"

"Well, one was an ace of hearts and the other was a jack of clubs. You see, that's what they call Blackjack. Except this particular blackjack we began calling a 'genuine Blackjack.' And it was genuine, too. An ace of hearts, and nobody had a bigger heart than ol' Blackjack, and a jack of clubs, a black jack. That's how we always knew it was ol' Blackjack who had come to the rescue. Everyone knew about the cards, and whenever anybody saw them, they immediately stopped what they were doing and cleared out. I'm talking about anybody who was up to no good, like those kids dealing drugs and the like. Nobody messed around with ol' Blackjack, I can tell you that."

"Did he have some kind of costume that he wore?" I asked.

Old Man Mobley leaned back and laughed. "Well, Keisha Johnson tried to make him a costume once," he said. "It was pretty nice, too. Black and green and all that. But ol' Blackjack finally decided he didn't want anything to do with a costume. Thought it was too flashy. He ended up keeping the black cape, though, I know that. Usually he wears just a black sweatshirt and green sweatpants. That, of course, along with his favorite sneakers. I think he had a special pair made once, like he needed it or something. Why, he could jump a skyscraper in slippers if he wanted to. And that's the truth, too."

I looked at Old Man Mobley, and then something came to mind. "Well, whatever happened to ol' Blackjack, does he ever come around here anymore?" I asked.

"Sometimes," Old Man Mobley said with a shake of his head. "Yep, he's still around somewhere, that I can tell you without any doubt. But, you see, now the authorities are looking for him, and, well, ol' Blackjack he didn't like that at all. No, sir."

"Did he do something wrong?"

"Well, like I told you, ol' Blackjack just wanted to help people. Anyway, we was just sitting there one day, when we hear this loud creaking. All of a sudden, Blackjack comes jumping over one of the buildings with an armored truck held above his head. Now I told you he was as strong as an ox, and I meant it, too. Well, anyway, he sets the truck down in the middle of everything, and starts pulling the doors open. I mean, can you imagine how strong ol' Blackjack was. He starts pulling the doors open, and then he says, 'This money inside is for the people who worked so hard during their lives and never made a cent. This money belongs to all the people and I mean to divide it so.' Then the doors swing open, and Blackjack heads inside. When he comes out, he's throwing money in the air to everyone who happened to be watching. Man, I never seen so much money in all my life. There's tens, twenties, and even hundred dollar bills flying through the air. Well, we reached up and grabbed as many bills as we could, that's for sure. Ol' Blackjack, he comes out with money in his fists, and starts handing it out to whoever he sees. Then he jumps up to the nearby windows, and starts throwing some of the money inside. It took hours before all the money inside that armored truck was gone."

"How much did you get?" I asked.

"Oh, a few hundred dollars or more," he replied. "Like I said, I knew ol' Blackjack since he was a little child. He kept on handing me bills, and I kept on taking them gladly. No telling when that money would come in handy. I remember how happy everyone was with all that money sticking out of their fists. When Blackjack finished, we all gave him a mighty cheer and then watched as he leaped over one of the buildings and disappeared from sight."

"Did you ever see him again?"

"Sure enough," Old Man Mobley laughed. "A few days later, we hear that creaking sound again, and then all of a sudden, ol' Blackjack comes jumping over that building over there with a huge food truck held over his head. I mean, we couldn't believe it. That boy had so much strength and agility, it's a wonder he wasn't holding the entire world over his head. Anyway, he puts the truck down and opens the doors, and starts handing out food to everybody. Well, you can just imagine how happy everyone was. That was our ol' Blackjack, all right. He starts handing out bread, meat, chicken, and all kinds of stuff. Why, it was enough food to eat throughout the year, and that's not all. No, soon he brings out all the chocolate and candy and cupcakes hiding inside. The children went wild, and we adults had a mind to go wild, too. People were walking around with all kinds of stuff in their arms. And you could hardly see their faces. All the time, Blackjack was smiling and laughing, telling the people that they deserved the food, and now because they wouldn't be hungry, they would be able to think up great thoughts to help gain the equality that was rightfully theirs. That Blackjack, mmm, he certainly was some piece of work, I can tell you that."

"Well, what happened to ol' Blackjack?" I asked.

Old Man Mobley frowned and shook his head. "You see, when he started bringing the trucks up here, the authorities started taking notice and they weren't too pleased. Blackjack was now hijacking all kinds of trucks: money trucks, food trucks, furniture trucks, department store trucks, and the like. The people were mighty happy, but the cops and those in charge thought of him as a crook. He was a crook all right, just like that Robin Hood you've heard talked about. Anyway, they decided they were going to stop Blackjack once and for all, and send him off to prison. Ol' Blackjack didn't take very kindly to that idea, so he decided that he would go away for a while until things calmed down a bit. I remember it was just around Christmas. Ol' Blackjack, he made sure to hang around for Kwanzaa before he took off. Yep, he sure did like that last Kwanzaa. "First fruits of the harvest," I think it means. Anyway, after the Kwanzaa feast, the Karumu, ol' Blackjack decided to leave. He told us he would try to make it back for Dr. King's birthday, but nobody has seen him since."

"Where do you think he went?"

"Can't tell you that," Old Man Mobley said. "But you should have been there when he left. He said goodbye to everybody, and then ol' Blackjack, he walked outside and leaped up in the air so high, I doubted if he would ever be able to come down again. And then do you know what happened? Of course, you don't so I'll tell you. Well, my friend, ol' Blackjack leaped so high he just stayed up there. I mean, he was flying! Now I know you're not going to believe me, but ol' Blackjack, he began flying away like a happy, big, black crow. Now don't ask me how, I just know that I seen it with my own eyes, that's all."

"And that was the last you saw of Blackjack?"

Old Man Mobley slowly nodded his head. "Haven't seen him since," he said with sadness in his voice. "But he's around, I know he's around. And I'm bettin' he'll be coming back this way again before too long. Anyway, Dr. King's birthday is only a few days away again."

I looked down, trying to think of something to cheer up Old Man Mobley, when I noticed something in his hand. "What have you got there?" I asked, hoping it would be something positive.

Old Man Mobley's eyes lit up. "Oh, these?" he said, holding up his hand. I could now see it was two playing cards, an ace of hearts and a jack of clubs. A genuine blackjack.

"Ol' Blackjack left me these before he took off," Old Man Mobley said. "Sure are beautiful cards, don't you think? Ol' Blackjack is sure to be back soon enough. Yep, sure enough."

That was the last I heard of ol' Blackjack. Everybody's expecting him to show up when Dr. King's birthday rolls around again, and this time, who knows what he'll be holding in his arms. As Old Man Mobley said, the older ol' Blackjack gets, the stronger and more agile he gets. If that's only somewhat true, who knows what Blackjack will do when he returns. He might just carry the whole projects off to some paradise or something. I know nobody living here would complain. I just wonder what the authorities would say about that. I guess it really doesn't matter, ol' Blackjack is too powerful for them, anyway. I'm just glad he likes helping people, man, or there would be tough times for sure. Anyway, Dr. King's birthday is coming. We all just hope it also brings Blackjack back to the neighborhood. Now that would really be something.

In the meantime, I bought a pack of playing cards. An ace of hearts and a jack of clubs are now pinned to the wall. That's a winning hand, all right. A genuine blackjack!

El Mozo

Let me tell you, amigos, the legend of El Mozo. You see, he was just a boy in a poor village when it all began. His family was among the poorest in the village, and El Mozo had hardly anything to eat as a boy. The people of the village were constantly abused and tormented by the wealthy landowners, who lived nearby in their huge haciendas.

Well, anyway, one day El Mozo decided he would go see Don Pedro Canalla, who was the wealthiest landowner, and try to convince him to be kinder to the people of his village. He really didn't think Don Pedro would listen to his pleas, but he decided he had nothing to lose. His people were already suffering so much that maybe Don Pedro did have a heart of some kind. Anyway, he would go see for himself. Things couldn't get any worse.

So El Mozo set off for the huge hacienda on the distant hill because he knew that's where Don Pedro Canalla lived. It would be a day's journey, but all El Mozo had was some bread and a small leather bag filled with water. This would have to be enough. So, anyway, El Mozo began walking from his small hut through his tiny, poor village. As he walked, he waved to everyone he saw.

When he reached the edge of his small village, he looked out across the landscape. He could not believe how big the world looked, and how rich the landowners in their distant haciendas were. Then he looked at the huge hacienda on the hill, and wondered what Don Pedro Canalla did with all his money. He sure didn't use it to help his people, he decided. Then El Mozo walked onward, determined to speak with Don Pedro and tell him the mistake he was making.

El Mozo kept walking. Through the fields and up and down the smaller hills that led to Don Pedro's hacienda. After climbing one of the small hills, he decided to sit down beneath a tree and rest for a while. He took a bite of his bread and drank some of his water, and then decided he would sleep for a few minutes. El Mozo closed his eyes, and then he thought he heard something moving nearby. He opened his eyes, and noticed a narrow column of light coming down from the heavens.

"This is surely a sign from God," he said to himself. "But what does it mean? I must try to find out."

El Mozo stood up, and began walking toward the column of light. Up above, he heard voices singing in praise of him.

"Oh, El Mozo, you are surely right to do this thing," they sang. "We have not forgotten your people. We will help you, El Mozo, so you can help your people."

El Mozo stood listening to the voices, and then kept walking toward the column of light. Amid the shadows and the light, he could see a brown horse standing near a bush. There were white patches on the horse's sides, and El Mozo wondered if he belonged to one of the landowners. Then he heard the voices above singing once again.

"This is what we have given to you, El Mozo," they sang. "Use it wisely to help your people."

El Mozo smiled, and walked toward the horse. But when he got close, the horse began running away from him. El Mozo followed the horse until they had reached the column of light. When the horse stepped inside the column of light, he stood there for a moment and then the white patches became huge white wings. El Mozo couldn't believe his eyes.

"What a beautiful horse," he said to himself. "A beautiful horse that can fly."

Then El Mozo looked up toward the heavens, and heard the singing once again. He then stepped into the column of light, and the horse did not move. He stroked the horse's cheek, and then stared at the huge white wings.

"Is this what you have given me to help my people?" El Mozo said, looking up above. When he heard the beautiful singing of angels, he smiled. "Then I will use this flying horse to give my people what they need," he said. "And as a tribute to heaven and scorn for hell, I will name him, El Diablo."

El Mozo looked up, and could see angels flying amid the clouds. Then the column of light suddenly vanished. He could no longer see any sign of the angels, and then looked at El Diablo. The horse was still standing there with its great white wings spread out from either side.

"Well, at least, you're still here, amigo," he said. "Let's go see Don Pedro Canalla, and see what he says about this great miracle. Surely, he will help the people now."

El Mozo climbed onto El Diablo's back, and then put his arms around the horse's neck.

"Fly, Diablo, fly!" he said.

The horse neighed, and then reared up on its hind legs. It then began flapping its huge white wings, and soared into the blue sky.

"I wish I had better clothes to meet with Don Pedro," El Mozo said to El Diablo. "And you had a beautiful, shiny saddle."

After a moment, El Mozo heard the singing once again. He told El Diablo to fly above the clouds so that he could see if there were angels there. El Diablo nodded his head, and the two of them sailed high into the air. Two clouds moved apart as they soared into the sky. When they passed between the clouds, the two clouds moved back together and El Mozo and El Diablo disappeared into the heavens.

Before too long, the clouds moved apart again, and El Mozo and El Diablo emerged into the blue sky. But things were very different now. El Mozo was wearing a white sombrero, and his old, ragged clothes were replaced with new white ones. On top of his new clothes, he wore a multi-colored serape. El Diablo, meanwhile, wore a brand new saddle with shiny silver stirrups.

"It is time to go see Don Pedro," El Mozo said. "He will surely listen to us now."

El Mozo and El Diablo flew toward the huge hacienda on the hill. When they got near, they could see someone standing on the veranda in a white suit. It was Don Pedro Canalla himself.

"Hola, Don Pedro!" El Mozo shouted. "And how are you today?"

"What business is it of yours?" Don Pedro replied. "And where did you get that horse?"

El Mozo told El Diablo to land on the veranda so he could talk to

Don Pedro. El Diablo, who was very smart, nodded his head and they sailed down to the veranda below. This was the first time El Mozo had ever met Don Pedro Canalla in person. He was a mean-looking man with a thin mustache, a pointed nose, and thick, black eyebrows.

"Ah, Don Pedro, it is nice to meet you," greeted El Mozo. "I have wanted to talk to you for a long time."

Don Pedro didn't smile. El Mozo could see he had a mean look in his black eyes. "You haven't answered my question," Don Pedro said. "Where did you get that horse?"

"He was a present from the heavens," El Mozo replied. "He was given to me so that I could help my people."

"And who are your people?" sneered Don Pedro.

"They are the people living in that village below your hacienda," El Mozo replied.

Don Pedro looked at him, and frowned. "Those are my people," he said. "They work for me, and so, if you come from the village, you also work for me. And, therefore, that is my horse!"

"No, Don Pedro, you don't understand," El Mozo said. "That horse was given to me by the angels—"

"Stupid dreaming peasant!" Don Pedro shouted. "Where did you steal that horse? Did you find him on my land?"

"No, he was given to me—"

"So you say," Don Pedro hissed. "Did you steal him from one of the other patrons?"

"No, he is my horse—"

"But he was on my land!" Don Pedro shouted. "Give him to me and I'll find out what to do with him."

El Mozo kept trying to explain how the horse was given to him, but Don Pedro wouldn't listen to his words. He finally threw the boy aside, and stomped toward El Diablo.

But I told you El Diablo was smart. When he saw Don Pedro come toward him, El Diablo flapped his great white wings and soared into the sky. Don Pedro was furious.

"Tell that horse to come back here," Don Pedro screamed. "You found him on my land, and he is therefore my property!"

"But he is not your property!" El Mozo shouted back. "He is mine, and he will stay mine!"

Don Pedro looked up at El Diablo flying through the air. He couldn't believe how majestic he looked flapping his great white wings. There was nothing in the world Don Pedro wanted more than that beautiful flying horse. And owned by one of his peasants? Bah, he would get him if it was the last thing he did.

Don Pedro thought for a moment, and then a crooked, evil smile appeared on his face. "But what was it that you wanted to talk to me about?" Don Pedro asked.

"I was going to ask you to help the people," El Mozo replied. "But now I see you have no intention of doing so."

"Not so fast," Don Pedro said. "How about if we make a deal? I will help the people if you give me that horse."

"That horse was given to me by the heavens," El Mozo explained. "I will never part with it. No deal!"

Don Pedro was so mad, his pointed nose turned red. Then his thick, black eyebrows fell toward his mean, black eyes. "He is no one's horse right now," he finally said. "I will get my shotgun and shoot him down. Then there will be no question as to who the horse belongs to."

"You would injure him for no reason, just to possess him?" El Mozo asked with fear and disbelief.

"Yes," Don Pedro answered. "Unless you decide to call him back here, and give him to me."

"Never!" El Mozo said.

"Then I will get my gun—"

Don Pedro turned, and went inside the hacienda. El Mozo knew this was his chance to escape, and he whistled for El Diablo. The beautiful flying horse suddenly sailed down to the veranda railing. El Mozo jumped from the railing onto El Diablo's back, and told him to fly away as fast as he could. The two of them soared into the blue sky, El Diablo's wings flapping quickly.

El Mozo looked back, and could see Don Pedro had returned to the veranda holding a shotgun. "Bring that horse back to me!" he shouted. "Thief!"

A shot was fired, but El Mozo and El Diablo were already high above the clouds. "So he will not help the people," El Mozo said. "Then I will do it myself, with your help, El Diablo."

El Diablo neighed his approval, and then the two of them heard the voices of the angels once again. They flew higher, hidden by the clouds, and then suddenly reappeared with a large leather bag hanging from El Mozo's shoulders.

"There is enough seed inside this bag to feed the entire village," El Mozo said. "All we have to do is get it planted."

He told El Diablo to fly down to the village, and as they soared downward, all the people came out of their small houses and waved their arms. When El Diablo landed, the people could not believe that it was El Mozo riding on top. They looked at his new clothes, and gasped.

"But El Mozo, where did you get that horse?" asked one of the young girls.

"It was a gift to me from the angels," El Mozo explained. "They said they wanted to help the people."

"It is surely one of God's miracles!" said one of the women. "And he has chosen you El Mozo to carry out his wishes."

"Yes," El Mozo said. "But Don Pedro Canalla refused to help you, so I have brought some seed to plant."

"We will plant the seed," one of the men said. "It was given to you from the heavens."

El Mozo then saw his mother and father, and his sisters and brothers, and they celebrated his good fortune. "Are you rich now?" asked his mother.

"No, but the angels want to help all of us become more fortunate," El Mozo said. "This seed was given to me by the heavens itself!"

"It surely is a miracle," his mother said.

Then El Mozo, his family, and the people of the village busily planted the seed in every patch of dirt that they could find.

"But it hasn't rained in weeks," said his father. "There's no way the seed will have a chance to grow."

"Do not worry," El Mozo said. "The angels will help."

As they planted the rest of the seed, El Mozo found a white wand on the bottom of the bag. Surely, this wand was a present from the angels. As he held it in his hands, he wondered about all the great things it could possibly do.

"I will use the wand to make it rain," he finally said.

The people still had a hard time believing El Mozo could actually make it rain, but when they saw him climb on top of El Diablo and fly into the air, their hope was renewed and they cheered.

"Anyone with a horse like that is surely favored by the heavens," someone said to El Mozo's mother.

She nodded her head, and smiled.

Meanwhile, El Mozo and El Diablo flew high into the clouds. As they flew inside one big, fluffy cloud, El Mozo waved the wand and asked the angels to make it rain. He heard the singing once again, and soon, the cloud turned black.

El Mozo and El Diablo flew back to the village. As they landed, there was the sound of thunder, and rain began to fall.

"Surely a miracle!" his mother said, as she saw the raindrops fall.

The people rejoiced, and before too long, plants of all kinds began to emerge from the soil and grow. There were soon vegetables of all sorts growing from the plants. The village was soon filled with green, ripe food.

"The angels surely favor you, El Mozo," said one of the men. "You are now more powerful than the patrons."

"The patrons," repeated El Mozo. "We must do something to free ourselves from their wealth and power."

He thought for a moment, and then smiled. He called for El Diablo, and they once again flew into the sky. Flying into another big, fluffy cloud, El Mozo waved the wand. "Please, dear angels, help us!" he said.

Very soon, the cloud turned black, and El Mozo and El Diablo flew back to the village.

"You're going to make it rain again?" his mother asked.

El Mozo smiled. "Just watch," he said.

There was soon the sound of thunder in the air. The people stood and waited for the raindrops to fall. But, instead of raindrops, gold coins began to fall from the sky!

The people cheered, and the children ran around the village picking up as many coins as they could carry. The men and women of the village also filled their arms and pockets with the gold coins.

"We are all rich!" a woman shouted. "Bless you, El Mozo!"

And that's the legend of El Mozo, amigos. It is said the village of San Pablo is now one of the richest towns in all of Mexico. And El Mozo?

Well, he and his family now live with El Diablo in a huge hacienda on a hill overlooking San Pablo. He continued to perform great miracles for the people, and he was loved by one and all — all, of course, except the landowners, who were furious that the people were now as rich as they were. El Mozo made sure this would be so, and the hill he chose overlooking San Pablo was the highest in the region – higher even than the hill of Don Pedro Canalla!

SUPERSTEIN

I AM THE MIGHTY Superstein, able to hurl matzohs at the speed of light and then explain what happened with the intelligent eloquence of an Einstein! Yes, I'm the mighty Superstein, who God has blessed with powers beyond those of mortal man! Yes, the mighty Superstein, able to travel through the air like a speeding knish and then part the waters of the Red Sea like Moses himself! Yes, the mighty Superstein!

"Irving! Get in the house right now!"

"Hark, there must be danger! I hear someone calling for help!"

"IRVING!"

"Are you in grave danger, my poor damsel in distress?!"

"The only danger, Mister Superhero, is your dinner getting cold if you don't come in the house right this moment!"

"Yes, nourishment for this mighty super body! Yes, endangered one, I'm coming as fast as I can!"

"Irving?"

"But I'm here endangered one, ready to save you from certain peril!"

"The only thing in peril is my patience, Mister Superman. What were you doing, anyway?"

"Saving the world for God and humankind!"

"Well, that can wait. Now sit down before your dinner gets cold. I don't want to have to tell your father about this."

"Yes, endangered one."

"The only thing endangered is your allowance if you keep up with this unholy charade."

"Unholy? But I'm on God's side, fighting for everything we believe."

"Yes, and He wants you to eat your dinner and take out the trash. If, Mister Up and Away, you can find it in your super schedule to do such mundane things."

"I have time for dinner, endangered one, but I'll have to eat fast."

"You want to get indigestion, Mister Out of This World?"

"No, but you see I'm due at the United Nations."

"Oh, I'm so sorry, I wouldn't want to keep all those ambassadors and diplomats waiting. You're still going to have to take out the garbage before you go. I'm sure they'll all understand."

"Yes, endangered one."

"You're going to be endangered, Mister Superhero, if you keep calling me that. Oh, good, your father's home. Maybe you can explain to him how you're saving the world for God and humankind. I'm sure he'll understand."

"Hi, Pop. Do you need saving?"

"Oh, boy, you don't know the half of it."

"Sit down, Marvin, your dinner's getting cold."

"What's with the boy?"

"Oh, didn't you know? Your son's a mighty superhero who's saving the world for God and humankind."

"That's nice. As long as he's keeping busy."

"I told him he had to take out the garbage before zipping off to the United Nations."

"I hope he's going to set those anti-Semites straight."

"Well, of course, you didn't think he was just going up there to sightsee, did you?"

"No, it's true, Pop. I'm the mighty Superstein—"

"Pretty cute, son, and you have a cape and everything. And a Jewish star sewn to your chest."

"Well, it's important to look the part, Pop. How else is anyone going to take me seriously?"

"I don't know, son, I think you have your work cut out for you as far as being taken seriously."

"But you don't understand. God spoke to me and told me He wanted me to save His world. He said He needed someone to tell everyone to stop fighting and get along with each other. That He had really had enough with all this monkey business and was ready to do another Noah job if we didn't listen."

"That's nice, son. What does your mother think?"

"I think he should start talking less to God and start studying more. Really, Irving, I wish you had more sense."

"Yeah, yeah. Well, I'm off!"

"Not before you take out the garbage, Mister United Nations."

"Yeah, yeah."

I am the mighty Superstein, and now I'm headed to the United Nations to finally put a stop to all fighting throughout the world! Like the Biblical Messiah, although I'm really not sure if I'm a legitimate descendant of David, I will bring peace to all nations in the name of God and humanity! Yes, I'm the mighty Superstein, who must now use his God-given super powers to fly across the sky and find my way to that institution that includes all nations of the earth! Away! Away!

"Where's Irving?"

"Why he's not back, yet?"

"What do you mean, Marvin?"

"I mean, he said he was going to the United Nations."

"Oh, that. Silly kid. But he really has to get some studying done."

"I'm sure he'll be back soon. I mean, how long can some ridiculous meeting at the UN last?"

"Be serious, Marvin. That boy's always goofing off. I think you should have a talk with him. Honestly, the boy's a little meshuganah."

"Oh, he'll grow out of it soon enough, Ida. I mean, it's not like he's hurting anyone."

"Really, Marvin, it's not healthy. I mean, he thinks he's Superman for crying out loud. You'd better talk to him."

Yes, nations of the world, it is I, the mighty Superstein! I have come to tell you that the Lord is not pleased with what's happening on this planet. He has asked me to come here to speak to all of you and demand that all war be halted immediately. It is time all of us on this planet lived in peace and harmony, and enjoyed all that this planet has to offer. This is not a request, but a demand! God has decreed it! We must stop warring immediately and destroy all of our nuclear weapons. It is imperative that God's demands be met! If not, he has assured me that this planet will be destroyed just like it was destroyed by the Flood in days of old! Listen to me, people! Before it's too late!

"He still hasn't come back?"

"Relax, Ida, he's probably playing with his friends."

"But he has school tomorrow—"

"You don't expect him to work all the time, do you? I mean, all work and no play makes Johnny a boring boy, or something like that."

"But really, going around thinking he's this Mister Superhero, do you think that's really normal?"

"There are worse things. He could think he was Jack the Ripper or something."

I am the mighty Superstein, having returned from the United Nations! The countries of the world have heard my words and they have agreed to listen! But my job is not yet done until all the nations of the world decide to live in peace and heed God's demand! Yes, I'm the mighty Superstein, and I will not rest until war has been banished from the land!

"Irving? Is that you?"

"Yes, my mother, I have returned!"

"It's about time, Mister Save the World. Don't you think you should be studying? I mean, this superhero thing is not much of a career."

"How can you say that? I'm doing God's bidding."

"Let God do his own bidding, Mister Save Humankind. He has nothing better to do. You, on the other hand, have school tomorrow."

"But I'm not finished yet."

"Oh, yes you are. Marvin, will you come in here and speak to him. It's time we put an end to this nonsense."

"But you don't understand—"

"I understand enough. Now go to your room!"

"But what about Mr. Kufor?"

"Mr. Kufor? Are you hiding someone there?"

"This is Mr. Kufor, he has joined me for further talks."

"Oh, hello. Are you one of Irving's teachers?"

"No, I'm not, ma'am."

"Marvin, could you come in here? Irving has brought home a black man to talk with us."

"A black man? What's happened, son?"

"Father, I'd like you to meet Mr. Kufor—"

"A pleasure. Now what's this all about?"

"Maybe you should tell them, Mr. Kufor."

"Irving Saperstein, if there's something going on that we don't know about—"

"Well, Superstein and I need to talk. He has brought up some very interesting points, and if I may say so, God is very distressed."

"Points? God? No, you don't understand. Irving has a very lively imagination—"

"No imagination, Mr. Superstein."

"But you've got to be kidding—"

"I do not kid, Mr. Superstein."

"But who are you and where are you from, anyway?"

"My name is Kufor. I happen to be the ambassador of the country of Ghana. I have come in the name of peace throughout the world."

"Then you mean?"

"Irving, why didn't you tell your mother about all this?"

"But I tried!"

"What are the neighbors going to say?"

"Does it matter, Ida, your son really is the mighty Superstein!"

"*Oy vey*! He couldn't be a doctor like the other boys?!"

I am the mighty Superstein, able to hurl matzohs at the speed of light and then explain what happened with the intelligent eloquence of an Einstein! All who hear me shall know peace, all who listen shall be led to paradise! For I am the mighty Superstein!

"Irving? There's somebody here who says he's from China!"

"I'll be there in a second!"

"A second and the world could be destroyed!"

"I'm on my way! For I am the mighty Superstein!"

"And you think it's easy being the mother of a superhero?"

"No, ma'am."

"No, indeed!"

THE THINKING ASYLUMS

WHENEVER ANYONE COMPLAINED ABOUT a problem vociferously enough, they were placed into large buildings called, Thinking Asylums. As life became worse and worse within the society, the asylums became quite crowded. One day, there was a report of an escape.

"We caution all our loyal citizens that a man of medium build and long, dark hair is at this moment roaming the streets of our fair society doing nothing but complaining about problems that have already been taken care of. Please stay inside and ignore him if you happen to see him. He is considered dangerous."

Jim Edmonds looked at his wife, Marjorie, as the warning blared from their television. A picture of a grimacing renegade flashed on the screen.

"Hope they find that maniac soon," said Jim.

"Yes, and before his melancholy spreads," said Marjorie.

There was suddenly a knocking at the door.

"Now who could that be at this time of night?" asked Marjorie.

Jim opened the door, and standing there was a man of medium build and long, dark hair attempting to catch his breath.

"Why, that's the man they're looking for," shouted Marjorie.

"Please," said the man. "Would you be kind enough to hide me?"

"No way," said Jim. "We've had enough of your kind."

"But how is it a crime?" asked the man, out of breath.

"Don't know," replied Jim. "But you must have done something. They don't put people in the asylums for no reason."

The man looked at them and frowned. "But you don't understand," he finally pleaded.

"It's not my job to understand," said Jim. "You better go back to the asylum before they find you." He then grabbed the door and slammed it in the man's face. "Damned complainers," muttered Jim.

"I wonder what crime he did commit?" said Marjorie, as Jim sat back down in front of the television.

"Oh, probably complaining about something that was none of his business," said Jim.

Through the streets, the man wandered pleading to be saved from the authorities. He was about to knock on another door, when a car pulled up to the curb. The doors swung open, and out stepped several officers.

"There he is!" shouted several people from their windows. "There's the man who escaped!"

The man turned, and began running down the avenue. The officers hurried in pursuit.

Women screamed, and people rushed to lock their doors. The man kept running until he spotted officers hurrying in the other direction. It was no use, he was surrounded.

"All right, halt right there!" shouted one of the officers, reaching for his gun.

The man frightened, turned towards the officer. "But all I said," he pleaded, "was that no war is a good war. That we must stop hating."

"That'll be enough," replied the officer. "Nobody wants to hear such baseless complaints. It is your job as a citizen to support anything your society decides is best for its citizenry. That's why you were placed in the asylum. You're a danger to the society." The officer looked at him and frowned. "You, my friend, are the worst kind of criminal. You think too much!"

Just then, the television cameras arrived. They set up their bright lights, and a female reporter stepped forward.

"Do you have anything to say?" she asked.

"I just think people should stop hating each other," said the man. "Stop killing each other for petty reasons that can easily be resolved. We should stop trying to hurt each other for selfish reasons, and try to embrace peace."

"Okay, that's enough!" shouted one of the officers. "Turn around and put your arms in the air."

The man looked at him, and fearing being returned to the Thinking Asylum, turned and began running away.

"Halt!" shouted the officers.

The man disregarded the warning, and kept running. A shot suddenly rang out and the man fell to the pavement. All of it was captured by the television cameras.

Jim Edmonds, who was watching it with his wife, turned to her and said, "Serves that maniac right. Who is he to criticize this country?"

WHEN THE ZOOKEEPER COMES

THE SUN SPARKLED IN the afternoon sky as two sheep stood in the emerald pasture waiting for the Zookeeper.

"When do you think He'll get here?" asked one of the sheep.

"Very soon," replied the other sheep confidently.

"You know they say when He finally does get here, the lambs will play with the wolves," said one of the sheep.

"You don't say," murmured the other sheep. "What a lovely thought."

"Yes, and all the animals from the past will return and we'll all live together in peace and tranquility."

"Where do you think He is now?" asked the other sheep.

"Oh, He's around. They say He's in the air, or maybe watching over us in the sky."

"So what makes you think He'll come down here? I mean, it sounds like He really has no need—"

"No need? Why, we're His creations and He loves us very much."

"How do you know?"

"Well, they say one of the animals talked to Him long ago, and He told him how much He loved everything and everybody and that He wanted us to live according to His rules."

"Where are these rules?" asked the other sheep.

"I'm not really sure, but they say one of the dogs knows where they are," said the sheep. "They say he's seen them with his own eyes."

"Does anybody know which dog it is?"

"Oh, he lived a very long time ago and passed them down to the other animals."

"I'd like to see these rules," said the sheep.

So they set off together across the green pasture until a large Old English Sheepdog came running towards them.

"And where are you going?" asked the sheepdog.

"We want to see the rules," said one of the sheep.

"The rules?"

"The Zookeeper's rules set down by one of the dogs all those years ago."

"You mean you've never seen the rules before?" asked the sheepdog.

"No, and we would like to so we know what to do until the Zookeeper gets here."

"They're kept by the hound in the barn," said the sheepdog. "He can show you the rules if you like."

They nodded their heads and bleated, and the sheepdog turned and led them through the pasture. When they saw the pigs lying in a mud puddle, they told them where they were going.

"We don't follow any rules," one of the pigs informed them. "We do whatever we like."

"But don't you even want to see the rules?" asked one of the sheep.

"Well, we ain't doing anything, anyway," replied one of the pigs. "We might as well come along if only just to be entertained."

So the pigs joined them, and then they marched on towards the barn. On the way, they spotted the goats.

"Don't you want to see the rules?" asked one of the sheep.

"Bah! Rules," answered one of the goats. "They're the rules of our oppressors."

"No, these rules were handed down from one of the dogs," explained the sheep. "Have you ever seen them before?"

The goats shook their heads.

"Well, then, why don't you come along and look for yourselves?" asked the sheep. "Then you can decide whether you like them or not."

The goats didn't know what to say, so they followed the sheepdog, sheep, and pigs to the barn. Outside the barn were chickens, ducks, and turkeys.

"We're going to look at the rules," explained one of the sheep. "Have you ever seen them?"

"Rules? Rules?" said one of the turkeys. "Yes, one needs rules."

"Then follow us inside the barn," said one of the sheep. "The hound is going to show us."

"Why, I wouldn't miss it for the world," said one of the chickens. "Lead the way."

So the sheepdog opened the door of the barn, and in marched the sheep, the pigs, the goats, the ducks, the chickens, and the turkeys. The sheepdog then called to the hound, who came running over.

"We want to see the rules, old boy," the sheepdog said.

"The ruuuuules?" replied the hound. "Oh, yes, the ruuuuules."

The hound followed the sheepdog into the barn, and then began digging around for the old book he had hidden inside. Hay and dust flew through the barn as the hound kept looking. He finally remembered he had buried it underneath the pile of hay closest to the barn wall. After digging for a few moments, he finally uncovered the small, black book.

"This was handed down throoooough the yeeears," said the hound. "It is what Dog said to the old retrieeeever years ago."

"Was that his name?" asked one of the sheep. "Dog?"

"Well, not rrrrreally," said the hound. "That is just how we referrrr to him."

"Well, what is his name?" asked the sheep.

"Why, he didn't say," explained the hound. "He said, 'I am that I am,' and came to be known as the Zoooookeeper."

"Very strange, if you ask me," said the sheep. "I bet his name really was Woolly Head—"

"Bah!" protested one of the goats. "His name must have been Horny Head."

"That's ridiculous," said one of the pigs. "His name must have been Mud Slinger. That would at least make some sense."

"I think his name was Old Quack," said one of the ducks. "Then the rules would make sense."

"We haven't even heard the rules, yet," answered one of the sheep. "And Woolly Head definitely was not a duck. Everyone knows he cares more about the sheep."

"I think his name was Mister Pecker," said one of the chickens. "He probably looked very much like a rooster."

"Names? Names?" said the turkeys. "Why, Gobbledy was his name. Yes, yes, of course."

"Woolly Head was not an awful turkey," argued one of the sheep. "I mean, could you imagine?"

"Bah! Horny Head wasn't a stupid sheep, either," said one of the goats.

"Old Quack!"

"Mud Slinger!"

"Mister Pecker!"

"Now, now," said the hound, trying to restore order. "The Zooookeeper is surely many things to many people. I like to think of Him as Dog, but they say He had a son who came down to the earth many mooooons ago. And they say this son was actually a monkey—"

"Monkey?"

"No way!"

"Ridiculous!"

"Well, that's what they say," said the hound. "And they say He did many great things."

"What great things?" asked one of the sheep.

"Well, He told everyone He had come to bring peace, and forgive everyone for the bad things they might have done here on earth."

"And was there peace?" asked the sheep.

"Well, no, not really," explained the hound.

"And what happened to this monkey?" asked one of the pigs.

"Well, they finally brought Him to the slaughterhouse," said the hound. "But because of this, the people were forgiven for the bad things they had done."

"Bah!" said one of the goats.

"And what was His name?" asked one of the sheep.

"He is knooooown as 'the Anointed One,'" said the hound. "And many believe He was the Zooookeeper's son and now lives with Him in the House above the clouds."

"Well, if He was Mud Slinger's son, He must have been a pig," argued one of the pigs. "The Anointed One' was probably anointed with mud."

"No, He was Woolly Head's son and a sheep," protested one of the sheep.

"Bah!" said one of the goats. "He was Horny Head's son and a goat."

"Old Quack's son was a duck," argued the ducks.

"Mister Pecker's son was a chicken," said one of the chickens. "There's no doubt of that."

"Gobbledy's son was a turkey," said the turkeys. "Yes, yes, a turkey."

"Well, whatever He was, many believe in Him," said the hound. "And they say He will cooooome back again with the Zoooookeeper."

"I do wish they would hurry," said one of the sheep. "We can't wait forever, you know."

"If He went to the slaughterhouse," said one of the pigs, "We will be waiting forever for Him to return. He's probably in the bellies of the Farm Masters."

"But His spirit lives on," explained the hound. "He was eaten all right, and so, He is inside of everyone."

"Bah!" said one of the goats. "So is my grandpappy."

"But when will they return?" asked one of the sheep. "We will wait for them if there's any chance that they'll come back."

"First, you must know the ruuuuuules," howled the hound. "We must live by the ruuuuules if they're ever going to return."

"And what are these stupid rules?" asked one of the pigs.

"Yes, tell us the rules!" shouted the sheep.

"Rules? Rules?" said the turkeys. "Yes, yes, the rules."

The hound opened the small, black book, and began to howl. "Ruuuule number one," he said. "There shall be no other Zookeepers but me!"

"We wouldn't think of praying to anyone but Woolly Head," said one of the sheep. "There would be no sense to it."

"Horny Head and nobody else!" shouted the goats.

"Old Quack!"

"Mister Pecker!"

"Yes, well, now that that's settled," said the hound. "Ruuuuule number two! You shall not make any images of me!"

"No images," repeated the sheep. "Only a duck with nothing better to do would do something like that."

"What? What?" screamed the ducks.

"No bowing or serving the Zooooookeeper!" shouted the hound, looking down at the open small, black book.

"Well, that's a relief," said one of the goats. "Horny Head knows that goats have a hard time bowing."

"Ruuuuuule number three!" shouted the hound. "Don't say His name unless you mean it!"

"That's one for the turkeys," said one of the pigs. "They'll say anything for no reason at all."

"What? What?" replied the turkeys. "Piggies!"

"Ruuuuule number four! Keep the seventh day holy!"

"And what day would that be?" asked one of the sheep.

"Ah, it don't matter," said one of the pigs. "Pick one."

"They all seem alike to us," said one of the turkeys.

"Ruuuuule number five! Honor your father and mother!"

"What a nice thought," said one of the sheep.

"Well, the Farm Masters don't honor them, that's for sure," argued one of the pigs. "Most of them are in the slaughterhouse."

"Ruuuuule number six! Don't kill anything!"

"Bah!" grumbled one of the goats. "I'd like to see what the wolves have to say to that."

"Question! Question!" shouted one of the sheep. "If we pick a flower, does that count as killing something?"

"Ruuuuule number seven! Don't mate with the other animals!"

"Really, now," muttered one of the sheep. "Woolly Head really is getting personal."

"You said it, baby doll," replied one of the pigs. "Why does Mud Slinger care who we mate with?"

"Ruuuuule number eight! Don't steal!"

"Tell that to the fox and the wolf," said one of the chickens. "Mister Pecker certainly knows what's been going on around here. I lose eggs all the time to those rotten thieves."

"Yes! Yes! Thieves!" said the turkeys.

"Ruuuuule number nine! Don't lie about the other animals!"

"That's a good one," said one of the pigs. "I wish everyone would stop saying we're dirty or something. Lies, all lies!"

"The fox and the wolf lie about us all the time," said one of the chickens.

"Liars! Liars!" the turkeys agreed.

"And ruuuuule number ten! Don't desire anything that is your neighbor's!"

"Well, that's an easy one," said one of the sheep. "Who would want the pigs' smelly, old mud hole anyway."

"Well, good for you, toots," answered one of the pigs. "I don't want your damned pasture, either. It's filled with bugs and pollen."

"And those are all the ruuuuuules!" howled the hound. "You must keep them always or you will never be favored by Dog—"

"You mean Woolly Head, of course," protested one of the sheep. "And we will keep His rules because He loves sheep most of all!"

"Bah!" said one of the goats. "Horny Head loves goats above all. We are the Chosen Ones."

"If anybody's chosen, it's us," said one of the pigs. "The Mud Slinger has always loved pigs more than anybody else. Why, I wouldn't be surprised if He was a real porker Himself."

"Old Quack loves ducks!" shouted the ducks.

"He loves the chickens!"

"Gobbledy loves turkeys," screeched the turkeys. "Yes, yes, he loves us!"

"No, he loves us!"

"He loves us!"

A fight soon broke out among the various animals. One of the pigs even found a firecracker on the barn floor and proceeded to blow up one of the ducks. The fight continued until all the animals had scratched or bitten the other animals.

"Everyone knows He loves us most of all," said one of the sheep, opening the barn door and walking back outside. "I wish I could ask Him."

The badly scratched hound followed her outside carrying the battered small, black book. "Why don't you pray to Him?" he asked.

"How do we do that?"

"Think of Him in your head. It's all done by telepathy."

Though the sheep didn't know what telepathy was, they nodded their heads and began walking to the pasture.

"Let's wait for Woolly Head in the pasture," said one of the sheep. "Then we'll surely be able to see Him when He returns."

"Yes, of course," said the other sheep. "Because He loves us most of all."

"And when He comes, the wolves will play with the lambs."

"What a lovely thought."

They stood standing in the green pasture for a few moments, and then one of the sheep looked at the other.

"When do you think Woolly Head will get here?" she asked.

"Very soon," the other sheep replied.

"Do you think He's watching us?"

"Of course," said the other sheep. "He cares about everything we do and say because He loves us very much."

"Yes, He loves us most of all."

OUT FROM THE DARKNESS

"HERBIE! HERBIE!"

Herb Reichlinger stopped running and glanced back over his shoulder. He smiled at his new wife, hailing him from their new apartment, and hurried onward. At seventy-five years old, he was determined to keep exercising his fit one-hundred-and–twenty-seven-pound body — if not for himself, then for his new wife. As the growing daylight glimmered across the pocked pavement, Reichlinger kept running. This was a new life, a good life, one far beyond the reaches of the darkness that had engulfed him over sixty years before...

Anschluss. He was eleven years old when the Nazis came marching into Vienna, Austria on March 13, 1938. The next morning the city was adorned with swastikas and Nazi flags. That was the beginning. That was the moment his world turned upside down and plunged into the darkness. Months later, on the night of November 9, 1938, that world was jolted by *Kristallnacht*, the "night of broken glass," when all over Germany and Austria, Nazi mobs murdered more than ninety Jews and demolished seventy-six synagogues. Another one-hundred-and-ninety-one synagogues were burned, as well as thousands of Jewish shops and businesses. About 30,000 Jews were arrested and sent to concentration camps. But what made *Kristallnacht* so frightening was that it was the first time in modern times that Jews experienced widespread violence in a western European country...

Herb Reichlinger never considered himself very religious. Most of his neighbors and friends were not Jewish, and as an only child, he didn't have much exposure to Jewish family life. He was apprenticing to be a baker of cakes when the violence first began, his family running a fruit store in Vienna. All that changed when the Nazis came marching into the city.

Juden raus! That was the dreaded Nazi phrase that reverberated throughout the European continent – Jews out! When Herb Reichlinger heard the phrase, his family hurriedly packed their bags and moved to Hungary. He would be safe there for a little while longer…

"Herbie! Herbie!"

Reichlinger looked behind him and could see his wife, Marilyn, attempting to catch up with him from behind. Reichlinger kept running through the sun-dappled street, all his worries and pain vanishing in the distance. He had buried one wife already and had helped raise two daughters. The future now seemed as bright as the hot Florida sun…

It was not always so promising. *Arbeit Macht Frei.* That was the sign placed by Rudolf Hoess over the gates of Auschwitz – "work makes one free." For Herb Reichlinger, it meant being taken and placed into forced labor when the Nazis marched into Budapest in 1943. He had been going to a school for Jews only, and now, he was beginning to understand what remained so obscure in his youth – he was Jewish, part of a culture disdained by the Christians of Europe for centuries.

From the Middle Ages, when Jews were thought to be in league with the Devil and blamed for the crucifixion of Jesus Christ, anti-Semitism had flourished throughout Europe. Many believed Jews were not human and that they used the blood of Christian children in their rituals. Then, in 1542, Martin Luther advocated burning synagogues and destroying Jewish houses. This anti-Jewish sentiment remained until the nineteenth century, when the Jews of Europe were finally granted equal rights to those of its Christian citizens. But it would not last long. Because of their significant role in the Industrial Revolution, Jews became associated with the evils of modernization.

By the mid-nineteenth century, a new theory of race had emerged. The Jews were promptly labeled a "lower" race. It was then political anti-Semitism began to spread. Anti-Jewish parties and organizations began to appear in Germany and Russia in the 1880s.

But World War I brought about an even more intense wave of anti-Semitism. Jews were soon associated with Communism. In Germany, Jews and Bolsheviks were regarded as enemies of the nation.

It was in this atmosphere that the Nazis took control of Germany. In addition to the fear of Communism, the economic depression of the 1930s left people wanting a stable government which could provide employment. They decided Adolf Hitler was the one who could carry out their wishes.

Aktion Reinhard, the code name for the extermination of European Jewry, began shortly thereafter. It was also known as *Endlosung*, the final solution. In the spring of 1944, Herb Reichlinger was taken to a labor camp in upper Hungary. Allied bombing of the area had intensified, and the Nazis were intent on destroying the Jews they had rounded up. Reichlinger had heard the reports of Jews being machine-gunned as he was transferred to several different towns in Hungary. His forced labor ended with a two-week "Death March" through the cold and snow.

He marched along with eight-hundred others with nothing to eat for about one-hundred-and-twenty miles. He glimpsed the ditches alongside the road containing the dead bodies of those who lagged behind or who tried to escape. There were random killings along the way, many carried out by Austrian civilians. About two-hundred-and-sixty-five people died on the two-week march. *Todesmarsche*.

When the march ended sometime during February of 1945, Reichlinger found himself a prisoner of the Mauthausen concentration camp in upper Austria. An estimated 120,000 people died at Mauthausen. Herb Reichlinger was not one of them. Because the camp was so overcrowded, Reichlinger and others were sent marching once again. This time, the march ended at another concentration camp, Gunskirchen. Herb Reichlinger was still wearing the clothes he had put on at home in Hungary.

"There were barracks, no bunks and no windows," says Reichlinger. "I was lying in the mud during the rain. People died like flies. They couldn't even bury all of those that died."

In the second half of April 1945, about seventeen thousand to twenty thousand prisoners were brought to Gunskirchen from Mauthausen and other camps. The prisoners did not work, they were too weak. Those that came to Gunskirchen just waited for death.

There was a ditch in the camp where the dead bodies were thrown. Herb Reichlinger saw his friends dying around him. "They were starving us," he says. "But word around camp was that the Americans were close by."

The Americans. Their last hope. Many, however, were already on the verge of death. Epidemics of typhus and dysentery abounded. There was one toilet for all the prisoners of Gunskirchen, and prisoners fought for a sip of the fresh water that was brought to camp once a day.

Then on May 4, 1945, the SS officers who ran the camp began to disappear. The next day, a United States Army Medical Corps unit arrived. There were 5,419 survivors, Herb Reichlinger among them. Reichlinger, however, was too numb to care that the Americans had arrived. He now weighed sixty-eight pounds, yet, still refused to eat. As the Americans handed out C-rations, Reichlinger watched as many of the survivors gobbled down too much of the food too quickly. Many of them died.

Herb Reichlinger finally ate the next morning. A meal of pasta cooked in milk. He had been taken by truck to the nearby hospital suffering from a case of typhoid fever. "It was heavenly to lie in bed," he was saying years later. "But it was tragic that after the liberation, so many lost their lives."

He very nearly became one of them. He was lying in a hospital bed with a temperature of 104 when he heard music wafting through the air. He listened to the music, and then suddenly felt as if he was floating above the bed. As he felt a strange feeling overtake him, Herb Reichlinger resolved to live...

Many of the others were not so lucky. Six million innocent people died at the camps. For most, their only crime was not believing in the majority's God. In all His infinite wisdom, God never bothered to explain to those in charge the errors of their ways. That a man was a man no matter how he addressed the omnipotent God. That, as Paul the Apostle once said, everyone had God whatever the rituals they engaged in. It was just another case of intolerance in the history of an intolerant world. The evidence of that intolerance lay silent across the European countryside.

There, the evidence remained. Auschwitz, where 1.1 million people were murdered; Belzec, where 600,000 were exterminated; Bergen-Belsen, where about 35,000 innocent lives were taken; Buchenwald, a German concentration camp where an unknown amount of people were killed; Chelmno, where about 320,000 people were murdered; Dachau, where an estimated 32,000 were killed; Dora/Mittelbau, another German camp where many were executed; Drancy, a French detention camp; Flossenburg, a camp near Nuremberg where the numbers of those murdered go uncounted; Gross-Rosen, a Polish camp where an estimated 40,000 perished; Janowska, an extermination camp in the Ukraine where many were killed; Kaiserwald/Riga, a concentration camp in Latvia where who knows how many were executed; Koldichevo, a camp in Belarus where about 22,000 were killed; Majdanek, where about 360,000 were murdered; Mauthausen, the camp in Austria where an estimated 120,000 were killed; Natzweiler/Struthof, a French camp where about 12,000 died; Neuengamme, where an estimated 56,000 were murdered; Plaszow, responsible for about 8,000 deaths; Ravensbruck, a camp near Berlin where many were killed; Sachsenhausen, another camp near Berlin where innocent people were murdered; Sered, a concentration camp in Slovakia where many died; Sobibor, a Polish camp where an estimated 250,000 were killed; Stutthof, another Polish camp responsible for about 65,000 deaths; Theresienstadt, a Czech camp where about 33,000 were murdered; Treblinka, a Polish extermination camp where the numbers of those murdered are unknown; Vaivara, a concentration camp in Estonia where it is not known how many were killed, and Westerbork, a transit camp in the Netherlands.

All of these places stood as evidence of the iniquity of the ages. The people who died there were victims of a systematic and indiscriminate slaughter. They had no weapons to defend themselves, a minority vastly outnumbered by those who followed a different religion. Most Europeans probably only knew Jews from the devastating reputation they gained centuries before after the Christian Savior walked the earth. A Savior of peace and understanding…

Herb Reichlinger kept running across the shimmering pavement.

He looked like any other runner making his way across the Florida landscape, the Nazi theory of race just a distant fiendish yowl.

"Herbie! Herbie!"

He looked back and smiled as his wife waved to him from behind...

Herb Reichlinger finally made it to a Displaced Persons Camp in Vienna. He was now one of many survivors known as *Sh'erit ha-Pletah* or "the Surviving Remnant." It was here that many of them attempted to locate family members or immigrate to the United States and Palestine. Herb Reichlinger chose the United States. He finally left for America in March of 1949. When he arrived in his new country, he was miraculously reunited with his mother (and learned that his father had been killed in the camps) and once again became a cake baker. He then was drafted into the Army and fought for the country that had liberated him...

Herb Reichlinger rounded a corner and headed back to his new wife waiting in the distance. He was retired now, and remembered fondly his long marriage to his first wife and their two married daughters. He had grandchildren now and a new life in the Florida sunshine. As he passed beneath the shade of some trees, he glanced into the sunlight. He could see his new wife waving to him in the glistening glare. His world had hurtled out from the darkness and back into a world of light, of hope.

Herb Reichlinger waved his arm, and smiling, ran until he reached his wife at the base of the steps leading up to their new apartment. He leaned forward, kissed her, and they walked up the steps holding hands.

Disappearing Act

It all started one morning, after he woke up and felt a tingling in his hands and head. His wife apparently didn't notice because she immediately turned an angry eye towards him, and let loose with a screeching combative barrage. That's when it first happened. He looked at her, shaking with disgust, and began shouting as loud as he could. "Go away!" he finally roared, flailing his arm in the air.

Before he could say another word, his wife disappeared, vanished. He stood staring at the spot for a moment, and then decided his eyes were playing tricks on him.

"Now where the hell did you go, Harriet?" he howled, looking around the room. "I'm not through with you, yet!"

But there was no longer any trace of Harriet anywhere throughout the house. He was still in the midst of searching for her when the kids woke up, and began screaming and running around.

"Well, I can't take this," he said, beginning to get angry once again. "Don't you kids have school or something?"

When there was no reply, he shook his arms and let them have it. "Be gone!" he roared, watching as they were about to send a vase sailing to the floor.

Miraculously, the vase never broke. Before the little varmints could push it off its stand, they had suddenly disappeared.

He stood staring at the vase, which had failed to topple, and scratched his head. Then he made another search of the house, but couldn't find a trace of either Harriet or the kids. He still didn't know what to make of it.

"Must have had some sleep last night," he muttered to himself. "Well, anyway, I have no time to worry about any of it, I have to get to work."

So, shrugging his shoulders, he grabbed his briefcase and lumbered out the door. "They'll probably turn up again," he said to himself, sliding into his car. "There's no way I could be that lucky."

He started up his car, and sped off down the highway, until he came to a large clot of traffic. After about twenty minutes of creeping along, he finally threw his head back, and began shouting.

"Be gone!" he roared, waving his arms in the air.

Before he could scream another word, all of the cars had vanished. As he surveyed the empty road, he let out a long whistle of disbelief. "Something must have happened during the night," he said to himself. "Something quite extraordinary."

Deciding he would try to figure out how it had happened later on, he stepped on the gas, and began cruising down the open highway.

When he reached the bridge, he noticed cars once again making their way into the city. He thought about what had previously happened, and smiled. "Maybe I can wish them all away," he said to himself. "Finally have some peace and quiet."

Stomping on his brakes, he screeched to a halt. As he heard the wailing horns blaring behind him, he shook his head and began to shout.

"Away, all of you away!" he roared, swinging his arms back and forth.

The sound of the horns suddenly died away, and he sat there studying the empty streets. "My God, it worked," he gushed. He then stepped on the gas, and sailed through the streets of the city without a car or person in sight. Somehow, he had made them all disappear.

"Wonder where they all go?" he mumbled to himself, pulling up to the empty curb. "Guess it really doesn't matter, as long as they're gone."

He strolled into his empty building, made his way to his empty office, and sat down, putting his feet up on the desk. "Well, I guess that's it," he announced to the empty room. "Nothing to worry about any longer, no senseless work to do anymore."

He sat back, and smiled.

He sat there for a few moments, and then another thought occurred to him. "What if I made everyone disappear?" he asked himself. "Yes, everyone in the world, that is, except for Karen Packer. Why, we could start all over again. And, this time, I'll personally make sure that the human race does it right. No more wars, no more greed, no more selfishness, just a happy brood living together in infinite peace."

He decided that, yes, that would be the right thing to do to save the world from hate and destruction. He, Dalton Treble, would personally save the planet from the excesses of human callousness.

He sat back, closed his eyes, and made sure in his mind that it was the right thing to do. Then he began to think of all the wars, the poverty, and the inhumanity of humankind. He began to get angry, and then began to shout.

"Be gone, all of you!" he screamed. "Be gone from my planet! All except Karen Packer!"

He opened his eyes, and smiled. It was done. The folly of the human race was finally over. Now, he and Karen Packer would begin again.

He slid back into his car amid the silence of the sprawling city. The streets, the cars, the massive buildings were all empty now. He would go back to his town and find Karen Packer, and they would never return to the large, empty city.

He started the car, and was soon speeding along the highway, watching the overwhelming emptiness soar past his window. When he reached his town, he found nothing but the empty houses and the wandering wind kicking up the last remnants of what the human race had left behind.

He was about to head back to his house, his wife, his children, when he remembered Karen Packer. Ah, Karen Packer. She had been the sexiest girl in high school, had developed at an early age, and had made all the boys gurgle with idealized aspirations. Karen Packer. And now she was his for the rest of his days. His Eve. The last time he had seen her was a few weeks ago at the grocery store. They had talked together, laughed together, and had decided to exchange phone numbers for a future dinner. He would bring his wife and she her husband. Now she was his.

He drove up to her house on the outskirts of town, and began searching for the one other person left alive in the entire world. He soon spotted her on her front steps sitting there crying.

"Karen!" he shouted, getting out of his car.

She looked at him with surprise, and then smiling, jumped up and ran towards him. He watched her as she hurried across her front lawn, knowing he had done the right thing. She was definitely the perfect Eve, with long blonde hair and a figure that would satisfy the gods.

"Oh, Dalton," she cried, "what's happened to everyone?"

He stood there thinking of a response, wondering if she could handle the truth. "I'm not sure," he replied. "But they won't be coming back."

"How do you know that?" she persisted.

"Because, oh heck, you might as well know the truth," he finally decided. "I wished them all away, all except for you and me."

She looked up at him, still confused. "But how could you do such a thing?" she asked. "I mean, how is it possible?"

"I really don't know," he answered. "But I woke up with a strange sensation running through my body this morning, and then when I got angry, I made my wife disappear."

"You bastard!" she shouted. "So it wasn't enough to destroy your own life, you had to destroy everyone else's, too."

"No, you don't understand. I only wanted to make the world a better place, start again, and make sure everything worked out right this time."

"Why did you leave me alive, Dalton?"

He smiled. "Because you, my darling, are going to be my Eve," he explained. "Together we'll make sure it all works out."

"But my husband, my kids, all gone?"

"I'm afraid so."

She lunged at him, tried to hit him, but he grabbed her arms and tried to make her understand.

"Now, I know you once said you would never make love to me unless I was the last man on earth," he said. "Well, now I am."

She looked at him and began to cry.

He finally did make her understand. The days passed, and when she was finally sure that he had been telling the truth, that her loved ones

171

and everyone else on the planet would not be back, she began to accept it. She even began to accept his plan for the future of the human race.

Then one morning he woke up, and decided he had been wrong about everything. While Karen was quite beautiful, she was even more annoying than Harriet. And the kids were more noisy and objectionable than the ones he had had with Harriet. In short, he was more unhappy now than he had ever been.

He was in the process of thinking things over, the future of the human race, when Karen stormed into the room and began shouting at him.

"Do you think you're a god?" she shrieked. "Well, I have something to say about that!"

He shook his head in disgust, and decided there was only one thing left to do.

"You're no god," she was screaming. "You're not even much of a man!"

He looked at her, and then began to shout back.

"And you're no Eve!" he said. "Why you're not good enough to start a race of chimpanzees!"

"Is that so?"

"Yes!"

She was picking something up, something heavy, and getting ready to throw it at him when he finally had had enough.

"Be gone!" he roared. "You and those nasty kids, get off my planet!"

Before the object in her hand could be sent whizzing towards his head, Karen was gone.

He stared at the spot where she had been standing, shrugged his shoulders, and headed for the stairs. There was no longer any noise anywhere in the house. He was alone. He stopped to listen to the silence, smiled, and then headed for the door.

He slid into his car, started it up, and drove off to no place in particular.